The Loch

The Loch

Published by The Conrad Press in the United Kingdom 2020

Tel: +44(0)1227 472 874
www.theconradpress.com
info@theconradpress.com

ISBN 978-1-913567-44-6

Typesetting and Cover Design by: Charlotte Mouncey, www.bookstyle.co.uk with painting by the author

The Conrad Press logo was designed by Maria Priestley.

Printed and bound in Great Britain by Clays Ltd, Elcograf S.p.A.

The Loch

Dee Taylor

PROLOGUE

The present time, somewhere in the Middle East

The man sat in the shade just inside the patio doors, his desultory gaze taking in the sun-baked swimming pool area and the view beyond, shimmering in the mid-afternoon heat haze.

He watched her sitting in a reclining poolside chair. How the years... and the vodka had taken their toll. She wasn't asleep, he knew that. She was alone with her thoughts behind the closed eyes and the sunglasses, her complete nakedness soaking up even more sun. What had become of the beautiful young girl he had first met so many years ago? God knows how much they had been in love then. His rheumy eyes watched her, seeing how the constant sun worshipping had turned her skin to something that resembled old leather, saw how her flesh had lost the firmness of youth.

Her fingers heavy with gold rings, nails painted red, clutched the ever present tall tumbler of vodka nestling in her lap.

He couldn't remember when they had last made love, even drunken sex seemed a distant memory.

He too was naked, but looking down he couldn't see his lap, it was somewhere under his ample gut. Lifting the bottle of Shlitz to his lips he sucked, gulped, then swore listlessly under his breath, directing his hate at the peroxided vision outside.

What had it all come to? This godforsaken country, the

interminable sun, the people, the food, the insects... and the mind-numbing boredom. They had sold their souls for a money belt full of gold, now the proceeds from that gold was all but gone, frittered away on this so-called lifestyle. This hopeless exile. He was dozing again, a fitful, boozed day dream.

As he fell into slumber, his mind floated away, back to the highlands. To the mountains and moors, the heather and bracken. It was raining. Beautiful soft, gentle, cooling rain. On his face, on the surface of the Loch.

CHAPTER ONE

THE SCOTTISH HIGHLANDS, MID-SUMMER 1967

The water surface lay like oiled black glass in the dawn light and a heavy mist hung in layers waiting for the June sun to burn it away. His fly, a black zulu, swished through the mist to plop lightly on the water, sending concentric ripples to scatter the midges from the surface.

'We're not doing so good this morning,' he looked round at her. She was kneeling over the Gaz stove. The delicious early morning smells of frying bacon and black coffee hit the nostrils in a special way in that pure highland air.

She laughed, 'thank heaven we weren't depending on you to catch our breakfast.'

'You just wait, I'm gonna get hooked into the biggest damn brownie you ever saw.' He chuckled and took a huge gulp of heather scented air.

'Oh boy, this is the life, what do you say, Teen?' He couldn't remember ever being so happy.

They'd met six months ago in a very different atmosphere to the one they were enjoying at the moment. The sunny loch-side setting, the towering mountains and high moors, and the sounds of children and holiday makers ringing in the pine scented air contrasted dramatically with the crowded, smoke filled dive in dock side Aberdeen.

He remembered the raunchy, thumping music, the cigarette

smoke hanging in the green and red spotlight, and the slim long-legged stripper gyrating to the driving sounds and the stamping feet of the pushing jostling audience of oil riggers.

He remembered what she looked like, what she was wearing that night, a tinsel gee string and silver thigh-high boots. He remembered her eyes, heavily shadowed and painted under false lashes, the way they stared out vacantly, almost unseeing, moving around the gawping sweating faces, defying their eyes, staring right back at them as she went about her work.

Like any other good-time girl in the wake of the North Sea oil boom, she'd known many men. Admirers from the rigs, pimps, gamblers and gangsters. Her lovers came from a cross section of this transient life. He remembered how intensely he'd fancied her and thought again about their first love making. The first time he'd experienced that beautiful, slim hard body, all his fantasies from the strip club coming true.

At first his ego was flattered when she'd started to fall for him, then gradually he began to see beyond her more obvious charms. She was intelligent, sensitive and good fun to be with. She'd been used to being pestered and pursued by every kind of riff-raff and dirty old man in Aberdeen and had begun to wonder over the last couple of years whether she'd ever find the right man to settle with. She'd always dreaded ending up like so many other strippers who had become totally trapped in that way of life and were still stripping when their biggest asset, their looks, had long deteriorated and the strip club circuit needed them less and less. With their looks fading along with their incomes, the inevitable would always happen… a gradual drift into full time prostitution.

She hadn't gone that far, but she'd been drifting around in a dangerous twilight underworld and was teetering on the brink of another degradation… the slow decline into alcoholism. She had been drinking heavily, a slow, steady increase in her intake over the recent years. Her looks had begun to suffer. She had begun to notice the slight puffiness in her face, the dullness in her eyes and hair. Her bathroom mirror had begun to tell its tale.

More disturbing though was the effect on her mind. At first there was a certain vagueness, a clouding of awareness, a difficulty to sort out truth from fiction in her day to day life, and reality from her night-time dreams. Then came the first blank… a complete, total and utter black-out of memory.

Waking suddenly… memories of only the early part of the evening, then nothing, just the staring up into the darkness of the strange bedroom, wide awake, pain hammering in her head. Sitting up in terror, then hearing the heavy breathing and smelling the stale sweat from the slumbering hulk beside her. The dawning of the sickening truth, she'd gone back to someone's flat and indulged in casual sex with a total stranger. The remorse was almost too much to bear. She would ease out of bed, gather up her clothes and shoes and creep out. On the way downstairs, a toilet to retch out her shame and the remains of the night's gin or vodka or whisky.

The bouts of 'Alcoholic Amnesia' as her doctor called them, became more frequent until eventually she would have a lapse of memory every time she drank. Now she would shudder when she thought of those days. She would never know how many times sex had been stolen from her while alcohol had run off with her mind.

Jack Armstrong had plucked her out of that nightmare existence. She'd prayed for the day when someone would come and save her. When he blurted out his feelings for her one drunken night, she'd grasped at the chance with both open arms. He'd had enough of the life he was leading and needed to settle down. She had listened enthralled while he talked for hours about his dreams of settling down far away from the North Sea and its oil boom. The more he talked, the more she knew her chance had come… her way out, her escape.

He watched as she sat on her haunches now and fiddled with the frying bacon. A tight red vest showing the hardness of her breasts in the morning chill, and the faded blue Levi 501s rolled up high over cowboy boots. The weather had been good to her, healing the marks of dissipation. Her fair skin had tanned to a gently freckled gold and her hair hung loosely and streaked with blonde. She looked the picture of healthy Scandinavian freshness. He thought and smiled as images of the lurid strip artist contrasted with this girl and their beautiful highland morning. However dark clouds had begun to appear on the horizon of their clear blue life together. Storm clouds of jealousy that would loom up in his mind. He'd seen and known her the way she'd been, and sometimes it was impossible to cope with the old images of their first meeting. Thoughts and questions about her past would seep into his mind, poisoning his feelings for her and eroding their happiness together. He knew there was no need to worry, he was sure of her feelings for him, but the slightest reference or comment would bring old memories crowding back, torturing him unmercifully. He'd try tentative questions, attempting to prise snippets of information about private experiences from her past. It was a compulsion, he hated himself for. She would try to be honest and her honesty would always cut through his heart like a bitter knife.

Gradually she had begun to dread the subtle interrogations. She had tried to help, but every discussion would end in tears, both hers and his.

Their relationship had become fragile, hanging on the slender brittle thread of her guilt and his jealousy. Their love for each other was still there but hanging by that thread. They had decided on a three-week holiday on the loch.

'A bit of camping and fishing will soon get our minds right,' he'd said.

They were having fun and there was still a great joy in their newfound freedom. But the intermittent traumas were still there, chiselling into the cracks. There were even times when her thoughts would wander in confusion, almost affectionately back to the Aberdeen dockside, back to the dubious friends, and the lurking faces of despair, and she would wonder whether they would ever work things out.

They'd made a truce after the last argument.

'Okay, okay… I promise, no more twenty questions, I swear.' He said solemnly holding up three fingers in a scout's salute. He had to hold her face up so she could see. He had reduced her to tears again. 'I'm sorry babe, I'm sorry. I love you very much, please forgive me,' he wiped both her cheeks with the palms of his hands. She sniffed, holding back her sobs, 'Remember you swore… you can't break the scout's law,' she said, smiling through the tears. 'Scout's honour,' he whispered.

Until a week ago they were both still in their jobs in Aberdeen. He had been diving professionally for ten years. Mexico, Africa, the Philippines and the Persian Gulf came before the North Sea.

He'd worked practically non-stop for the past three months, pipe-laying at terrifying depths of three hundred feet. The money was good, £2000 a week plus bonuses, that was good for 1967, but the conditions, the worst in the world, made up for it. When the three months were up, he'd had enough, besides he'd met her. They would settle in Cornwall. He would get a small freelance diving business underway. Salvage, treasure hunting, that sort of thing. Although he had spent wildly on shore, he'd still managed to save enough to enable him to buy a small cottage and get a business going. The idyllic dream had to come true for them both.

He watched the water surface carefully for signs of trout rising, decided on a spot and flicked the zulu again... plop... he waited for it to sink.

'Hey, come on, give up for a while, maybe breakfast will make you do it better.'

'Sssh... I have a feeling this time,' he joked.

He watched the line snaking along the surface willing a fish to take. It twitched, then straightened, and he felt the fish.

'What did I tell you!'

The rod tip arched violently as he struck, then twitched and bucked and tremored... suddenly it was a thing alive. That feeling of a good fish fighting hard, sending shock signals up the line, along the rod to his hands could never be equalled, it was like the first time. The sensual excitement never diminished.

She dropped the fork and ran over.

'Landing net!'

'Ok got it,' she stood by him, the net in the water, like he'd taught her, waiting for him to guide the trout over it.

'This little fella really is kicking up a struggle, I reckon a three pounder.'

'I can't see it yet,' she squealed.

Suddenly a swirl, and the dorsal fin showed for a second… then out it came, clear of the water, shuddering to rid itself of the fly that was biting into its jaw. A split second and it was gone, boring deep, pulling the rod tip down almost to the water surface.

'He's big!' her voice shrill like a little girl's.

'He's tiring now, get ready with the net, I'll bring him up.'

He pumped him up to the surface again, they could see it now, shaking its head from side to side, swimming zig zag, looking a bit subdued but not giving up.

The fish was about three feet from the net when the huge rocket shape flashed suddenly from a clump of reeds almost under his feet. Like a bullet it homed in and hit the trout. She screamed, he almost dropped the rod as he lost his footing and stumbled into the water. There was one violent tug, the clutch screamed, then nothing.

'Shit did… did you see that?'

She was standing there, her hands to her mouth. He looked down at his drenched shorts, then at his rod, limp now… no more life in it, then along to a spot less than three feet away on the pebble bottom. His beautiful brownie lay, mouth gulping, eyes staring, gills working but wrenched in half amid blood, white membrane and loose scales.

'A pike, did you see the size of that bastard?' His heart was pounding. She was laughing now, for a split second he felt anger, frustration… then he too was laughing. She splashed across, they collapsed into each other's arms and sat down up to their chests in Loch Ness.

'I'm gonna catch that thieving bastard now, if it's the last thing I do, he must have been at least 15 pounds, did you see him properly?'.

'Yes darling, I did, I did, but right now we are having breakfast, then we'll get him.'

An hour later he was setting up the pike tackle while she fished for live bait to his instructions. This time float fished lob worm was bringing in slender 9" trout quickly and easily. She'd already dropped three into the keep net. His pike tackle was just as simple and to the point. A big orange float, seven feet up from a wire snap tackle of two treble hooks.

The live-bait hung limp and quivering by the two hooks. He folded back the bale arm on the big fixed spool reel and lobbed the live-bait out with a slow, gentle sideways cast. Float and live-bait landed about ten yards out with a splash. The trout sank beneath the surface and lay inert for a full five seconds, hurt and shocked by its crude and painful flight through the air and the awkward splash.

Then it started to struggle, flicking, shuddering, wriggling and tugging against the hooks impaling it. They watched the float suddenly bobbing and skittering over the surface, suddenly it was a thing alive.

'Wow, look at it go!' She breathed.

He carefully placed the rod into two rod rests, leaving the bale arm back, exposing the two hundred yards of line, leaving it free to run when the pike struck. A huge pike like the one he was after would strip off yards of line before it would give up and come to the gaff or net.

She moved over and put her arm in his, snuggling up

with anticipation.

'What are we going to do with it when we catch it? We can't eat all 15 pounds ourselves.'

He giggled. 'You don't catch pike for eating stupid, not in this country anyway. They get caught for kicks, for sport, then putting back. Some people stuff them and stick them in glass cases, but they are an essential part of the natural balance and shouldn't be killed. Mind you, I think pike is a delicacy in some countries.'

Suddenly the float disappeared with a plop.

'What's that?' She breathed. Then it reappeared, his heart skipped a beat too. 'No, that was just an extra big struggle, you'll soon know when the pike takes.'

The pike was swimming just beyond where the shallow pebble bottom suddenly shelved off into the abyss. Steep and sheer the shelf plunged, down into the darkness. Seven feet below the surface the live-bait swam frantically to and fro along a wall of rock overhangs and crevices. The visibility here was about ten feet at the most. Below was a green darkness out of which long strands of weed reached up out of the dark.

Big predators are lazy. They prefer to lie in ambush for their prey and wait for them to swim past their jaws. Normal under-water vibrations such as small swimming fish will stir them out of their lethargy. There is another kind of vibration, the shock signals of distress, agonised signals like the ones radiating from the impaled trout. The messages of fear and pain will stab through the brain of a sleepy predator, even one that has just gorged to its fill, and ignite the frenzy of a wanton killer.

The big pike lay above a weed festooned rock overhang about seven feet below the struggling live-bait. It lay with most of its length hidden in the foliage. Its huge bony head protruding, shovel like jaws opening and closing fractionally as the gills worked, exposing glimpses of killer teeth. The green eyes fixed on the struggling live-bait in a glazed and baleful stare. Slowly it slid forward from its lair, the massive speckled girth tensing into attack. Then, it stopped and retreated into the weed... a new vibration, a new danger signal. A great fear coursed through the pike's flanks... the predatory urge draining instantly. Something moving below in the blackness, an awesome new presence. A gigantic bulk approaching, ascending from the depths and through the weeds. The pike withdrew completely, the tip of its snout only exposed, jaws working faster with fear.

'Something's happening I think.' They watched the float suddenly change the pattern of its dance.

The live bait was crazy with fear.

'The pike is very near now,' he said, grasping the butt of the rod. 'Get ready, we've got a fight on our hands any second now.'

The pike felt the surge of water pressure, it cringed as the gargantuan mass moved slowly passed within inches. The float disappeared.

'Right, this is it. Gotta wait a few seconds now for the pike to turn the bait in its mouth before swallowing.'

The next few seconds would be etched on their memories for the rest of their lives and would change their lives forever.

The water around where the float had been seemed to rise up in a huge smooth mound, then suddenly exploded like an under-water bomb.

Her scream choked in her throat as the head and back broke the surface. The next five seconds erupted before their eyes like a vision from a nightmare. A great surging, swirling vortex, a glimpse of something that could have been a fin or a limb, a rolling dive, a flash of yellow underside, then it was gone. Nothing again, nothing except a few frothy bubbles on the surface and a pervading fishy, animal stench.

They both stood there, hearts pounding, hands trembling, blood drained from their faces.

He was shaking uncontrollably, she was crying.

CHAPTER TWO

'*Around twelve thousand years ago, back into the primeval mists of time, gigantic ancient glaciers slithered across and sliced Scotland in two. From Inverness and the North Sea, to the south and Fort William and the Atlantic. A jagged gash slashing diagonally from North Sea to south west, nigh on a thousand feet deep in places and a mile wide. This incredible chasm lay ice-bound for centuries. Then the ice age loosened its frozen grip. Centuries went by, prehistoric earthquakes rocked the highlands, literally moving mountains. The land slid and ground against itself along this fault line until eventually sealing itself north and south. So a great inland sea became landlocked within its own deep valley. The Great Glen... Loch Ness.*

Gradually the seawater changed to fresh. Whatever sea creatures remained trapped either died out eventually or evolved and adapted to their new environment. The loch is now a perfect natural aquarium. Deeper even than the North Sea, it is fed by numerous mountain rivers and small burns which bring oxygen and fish. The waters of the loch are dark and murky, with the visibility never more than a few feet at the surface, and black as night in the depths. This is caused by millions of peat particles brought down by the rivers and burns that feed the loch. Salmon and trout abound in great numbers, huge pike, perch and a few other freshwater species to a lesser degree, and millions of deep water arctic char, and in the slimy blackness of the great depths, a massive population of common eels.'

She was lying with her head on his chest, one leg drawn up across him. He was reading to her from a guide book about the Scottish highlands, the light of the hurricane lamp washing them in a secure warm glow, secure from the eerie highland night, the dark loch only a few yards away, and the denizens lurking in its waters.

He yawned, 'I can't read any more, I'm dead beat.' He reached over and put the guidebook onto the camp table.

'I don't think I'm going to be able to sleep, I just can't stop thinking about it.' Her voice sounded frightened. He drew his arms tightly around her and she snuggled deeper into him.

'Do you think it's something that could come out on land?'

'Hey, come on now. Of course it can't, have you ever heard of anybody seeing the Loch Ness Monster out for a stroll?' He chuckled but knew that he was wondering the same thing himself. He remembered reading somewhere about a supposed authenticated sighting that took place in the thirties. A man, Mr Spicer and his wife had supposedly seen a huge creature actually crossing the Foyers Road, the very road they were now camping under.

'Don't joke darling, please, I don't think I'll ever get over what happened today, I'm really scared.'

'We must count ourselves lucky, look at it that way,' he said drawing her closer.

'We now know for sure that there is something in there... we've seen it with our own eyes. I want to find out more about it.'

'OK, but are those tent flaps securely zipped?' She shrank even further down into their double sleeping bag.

'Yeah, yeah, don't worry babe, you're safe with me, get some sleep, I wanna get up nice and early in the morning, there's a lot of things to do.'

'What do you mean?'

'Now listen, do you realise, if the circumstances were a bit different, say we had a little more time, say perhaps the thing stayed around a little longer, and say we had the camera ready, OK, I know there are a lot of ifs, but if we had managed to get a shot of it at close range, and provided the photographs came out OK... we could really be in the money.'

'What you mean, sell the picture to the newspapers?'

'Yeah, why not. As far as I know there never has been a completely authenticated and convincing photograph that proves to the world beyond doubt that there is something unusual in the loch, the discovery of a yet unknown species. The papers would pay handsomely for a really good picture, I mean one that proves it once and for all.'

'But surely there've been hundreds of people who have spent a lot of money and time already and come up with nothing.' She could sense a fear within, not a fear of the loch's monster, but a fear, and uneasiness for herself, for their future... for her future.

'Yeah, that's true, lots of people, especially in the last few years. There've been TV sponsored expeditions, outfits with sonar and other highly specialised and technical equipment, and even some nutcase with a miniature submarine.'

'Wasn't there a Japanese expedition last year, they had a submarine as well I think.' Her voice was beginning to sound drowsy.

He wanted to keep the discussion alive. 'And there's the Loch Ness Zoological Research Bureau stationed on the loch.

Apparently, they keep a round the clock watch with powerful telescopes and movie cameras set up ready to roll. They've been on the loch for a few years now.'

'Have they spotted anything?' She yawned drowsily.

'I'm sure they have... boy, the whole thing has really got me going, I wanna find out as much as possible about the bloody thing. We'll pop round to the Bureau's headquarters first thing in the morning, they must have a lot of info, it'll be a good start anyway.'

'A good start for what? What are you cooking up? Remember what we're supposed to be doing darling... I gave up a perfectly respectable job to go down to Cornwall, get married and set up home. We are only supposed to be stopped off here for a couple of weeks.'

He laughed, 'I'm sorry Hun, maybe I'm obsessing a bit, we'll go see what there is at the Bureau, as I say, the thing we saw has really got me going, but don't worry, we'll be on our way south just like we planned.'

'We'd better, otherwise I'm going right back to my respectable job. I don't want anything more to do with that ghastly... whatever it is.' Her words brought familiar feelings to nag at the back of his mind. Did she mean that, was she secretly wanting her old life back? He shoved the thought from his mind.

'OK, but remember, we're most probably the only two people in the world who have seen the Loch Ness Monster at close quarters. We can't forget all about it just like that.'

She yawned again, 'well look what happened when you rang the newspaper this morning, they practically laughed at you.'

'I know, but how can you blame them, we had no proof. They must be inundated with calls every summer, and most of them from cranks. They want proof, and the only real proof is a first-class photograph, sharp and at close range.'

'Of course, the best thing of all would be to capture it.' She yawned a sleepy chuckle from under her pillow.

'Why not, we were only a few feet from it this morning, we know it goes for live fish, I don't see that the idea is such a joke.'

'Oh, shut up and go to sleep.'

They lay silently for a few minutes, then the Loch Ness night crept in and enveloped them in slumber.

Outside the tent the trees and boulders on the steep sides of the great glen crouched like silent brooding monsters in the gloaming, that eerie twilight that lurks throughout the night during a highland summer.

Dark shapes moved under the trees on the water's edge. The deer, fox and badger at peace from the daytime hordes of tourists, caravaners and coach parties. A long-eared owl called from the timber above the Foyers Road, or perhaps from the ruined turrets of Urquhart Castle across the loch. Then a larger bulk moving near the tent entrance, a snout, then sniffing and heavy breathing along the tent edges.

The early morning sun on the canvas was warm enough at 7:30 to make the inside of the tent almost stifling. She was still clinging to him and the sweaty closeness had woken him in mild claustrophobia. Her breathing was still deep and steady, so he decided to get up and organise the breakfast as a surprise. Extricating himself from her entwining legs and arms with great care, he pulled on a jumper and jeans and crept out into the sharp sunlight and noticed how deceiving the tent warmth was.

The air was crisp, and mist still clung heavily to the loch

surface and around the campsite. He couldn't help but look at the spot in the water from which the creature had burst, half expecting to see that terrifying vision, that tumult, of confused images… the huge, swirling bulk… and that smell! He scanned the loch and thought that even if there was something out there, it would be hidden by the thick mist that lay on the surface like a snowfall. A twig snapping and the sound of heavy boots on loose rocks made him spin round with a start.

'Good mornin' neighbour.' The loud greeting startled him. Two men were standing a few feet to the right of the tent.

'Good morning.'

They were both standing there grinning, both carried unbroken shotguns, a german shepherd slunk at their heels, ears back, tail between its legs. He didn't like what he saw and felt instantly apprehensive, afraid, for himself and for her lying naked and asleep only a few feet from them. Their vibes were bad, a threat to their happiness, their holiday, their new adventure. He thought of his own twelve bore inside the tent.

'We're lookin' for our horse, you ain't seen it I suppose?' The voice was coarse, a rough rural accent he couldn't identify, but definitely not Scottish, there was no trace of the gentle lilt of the highlands.

'No, I haven't, I'm sorry.' A sense of relief now that he knew what they were after.

'Yeah, we had 'im hobbled, reckon he broke the bloody hobble again, he's a bleedin' nuisance, always runnin' away.'

'Ahh…' one of them bent down by the tent. His heart missed a beat.

'Yeah, he's been 'ere alright… hoof prints, and he's been chewing grass round your tent 'ere.'

'And shittin' as well.' The other chuckled hoarsely, pointing to dollops of fresh dung.

'The bastard, wonder where he's buggered off to now, wait till I git me hands on him.'

He noticed how rough they looked, real pikey types. The one kneeling by the tent must have been in his mid-twenties. He wore an army surplus bush hat pulled down over his eyes, his complexion was fair but reddened by sun and wind, and his hair hung on his shoulders in greasy blonde strands. He wore a red neckerchief and faded but dirty denim jacket, and jeans that were too short, showing off worn down old cuban heeled ankle boots, the type with zips up the insides. His hands were big and dirty, stained badly with nicotine. Armstrong half expected to see 'Love' and 'Hate' tattooed on the fingers. The other one stood at least six feet four inches and was heavy with it, perhaps fifteen stone or more, at least five stone heavier than his mate. He wore a tattered sheepskin jacket and old woollen tartan trousers tucked into his wellingtons. His features were fleshy and ruddy, covered with several day's growth of dark stubble. His head was bare and cropped to the same length as the stubble on his chin. A brass ring in his right ear added that final little touch to his beauty.

He strode over, hand outstretched. Armstrong saw piggy eyes, too close together and yellow stained teeth.

'Names Barsh, Charlie Barsh... this 'ere is my brother, Loon. He ain't got that name for nothin.' Charlie giggled. Loon grinned insanely.

'Yeah... my name's Loon.'

Jack expected a vice-like grip but got instead a clammy loose up and down sort of a handshake. He felt like wiping his hand on his jeans after it.

'You called me neighbour?'

'Yeah, we got a caravan over on the other side of them trees.' He pointed south along the bank to some heavy timber reaching down to the water's edge.

'You campin' here alone?' The thinner one was looking towards the tent.

'Err... no, my girlfriend is asleep inside.'

'What, you holidayin?'

'Yes... taking a well-earned break from hard work.'

'Anyways, if there's anything we can do fer yer, let us know.'

'Yes, thanks a lot,' he watched them walk off along the bank.

'Who was that?' He lifted the tent flap, irritated that she'd woken before he could get the breakfast. 'Oh, a couple of fellas living along the shore a bit.' She looked snug and inviting, curled up among the blankets and pillows on the double camp bed.

'Come in and give me a cuddle.'

He knew he couldn't resist.

Two hours later they cooked breakfast.

The Loch Ness Zoological Research Bureau was a collection of three caravans huddled together on a huge layby on the Caledonian Road overhanging the steep 200 feet drop to the loch. Temporary slip roads gave access to a car park for the constant flow of visiting coaches and cars. The Bureau was set up by a private American syndicate using the casual help of students, freelance zoologists, and any serious enthusiasts on a full or part-time basis. The idea being that a constant round-the-clock watch be made on the loch in shifts, manning the movie cameras and telescopes, mounted not only at the site, but at various strategic vantage points around the loch.

By eleven o'clock the sun was already high, fulfilling its early morning promise of another gloriously blazing June day. Their yellow beetle turned off into the slip road and crunched to a halt on the cinders of the car park.

'Wow just take a look at that view!' She squealed, walking over to the railings.

The loch reached out on either side, disappearing miles away into the distance along the Great Glen.

'Gives you some idea of the size of it. What we're looking at now is only a part of the loch. It's actually twenty miles long… as long as the English Channel is wide.'

There was hardly a breath of wind, and the water surface from that height looked glass smooth. A small boat was moving slowly up the middle of the loch leaving a wake that spread in a giant V, the ends reaching almost to both banks, a mile on either side. They could hear the faint chug, reaching their ears long seconds after leaving the engines.

'That could easily be the monster from this distance,' she said, shielding her eyes with her sunglasses.

'Yeah, apparently most supposed sightings turn out to be boats. Look at that wake, no not near the boat but way back, at least a mile from the boat about there.' He pointed to one of the ends of the V. 'If we were standing on the shore over there, we wouldn't realise a boat had been past long before, and that wake would be totally unexplainable to us, especially at water level. Come on, let's go take a look at what these people have got.'

The longest caravan had a big sign running along the top of it, announcing in big black capital letters 'THE LOCH NESS ZOOLOGICAL RESEARCH BUREAU'. At the door, another sign, 'EXHIBITION Way in'. Inside the door was a student-looking girl sitting at a table selling admission tickets. The rest of the interior housed the exhibition. All the walls were covered in photographs, diagrams, maps and statistics. There were a few free-standing displays with big blow-ups from photographs. There were trestle tables with books, pamphlets and brochures of all kinds. A huge blow-up of two humps and what looked like a neck attracted her attention first.

'God, look at that!' She grabbed his arm, pulling him towards it.

'Hey, cool it, don't be impatient, let's start at the beginning and work our way round.'

They spent the next hour enthralled by the amazing wealth of photographic evidence before their eyes. There were humps, necks and tails, water disturbances and wakes of all kinds, and from all angles. There were maps of the loch with coloured pins indicating sightings, cross-sections of the loch and diagrams of various technological experiments.

'Look!'… She pointed to a cross-section diagram of the loch with the Eiffel Tower and St. Paul's Cathedral standing on the bottom and completely submerged.

'That really brings it home, wow!'

'Boy, I never dreamt there was this amount of photography taken of the creature.' She whispered.

'Yes, but tell you what, none of these pictures show the monster as close up as we saw it. Shit, if we had a camera then, our picture would have been a sensation. All these pictures are

27

either too far away or out of focus, or the wrong angle or something. Ours would have been definite proof once and for all.'

'Excuse me sir,' they both looked round, 'did I hear you mention a sighting?' He was a tall slender young man with an American accent, a pleasant bearded face, a navy-blue roll necked jumper, faded Levis and sandals.

'Yes, we saw it yesterday.'

'My name's Bell, Jimmy Bell. I try to run all this, tell me more.'

'My name's Jack Armstrong, this is Tina.' They shook hands.

'Come and sit down and tell me all about it.' They walked over to a table and chairs in one of the corners.

'Now, from what I overheard, it sounds like you had a really close-up experience.'

'If you reckon ten yards is a close-up experience, yes.'

'You're joking,' Bell leaned across the desk intently, 'you mean the creature broke surface as close as that to you?'

'Yes.'

'Where were you, in a boat, fishing…?'

'On the bank fishing,' she said.

'It sounds like you've had just about the best sighting ever,' he turned and slid open a drawer in a cabinet behind him.

'A sighting like that is what we people have been looking for since 1960 when all this was first set up.' He got out a buff coloured form. 'Right, this is a form we fill in when we feel a sighting is worth documenting, so can I ask you for more details?'

'Yeah, sure.' They hadn't expected to be taken so seriously, especially after yesterday's reaction from the local press.

'Right, first question, any independent witnesses?'

'No, just ourselves.' He looked disappointed.

'Yes, I thought so, that's always the biggest problem. No witnesses mean the sighting cannot be documented as genuine, all we can do is file it for our own purposes.'

'I suppose you get hundreds of hoaxes.'

'Not so much hoaxes, but you wouldn't believe the amount of people who think they've seen something. With the thousands of tourists every year, none of them knowing anything about the loch, all kinds of things get mistaken for the creature. We have a list as long as your arm of the kind of things that, given the right light, right angle, nature of water surface, can look, even to the experienced eye, unmistakably like a monster.'

He pulled out a 10' x 8' print of water surface, with something that looked like a hump. Then another print, this time of a fishing boat taken in mid-loch. He laid the pictures side by side. 'The hump picture is nothing but a close-up blow-up of a section of this picture,' he pointed to part of the wake from the fishing boat.

She looked at Jack, remembering the big V shape.

'The camera caught that wake just as the light was hitting the water in a special way,' Bell said, 'unless one has spent years looking at water, getting used to water surface, current pattern, the trick light plays, you can make an awful fool of yourself, especially around Loch Ness.'

'What we saw was no illusion, I promise.' Armstrong said.

'I know that, I believe you, I believe one hundred percent in the creature. It's my whole life. But the press and scientific world don't want to believe until there is absolute proof. They want to make fun, laugh at the creature, that's why we're here. I've dedicated my life to ramming all their stupid copy and funny Nessie cartoons down their throats one day. OK, let's carry on with the questionnaire.'

The questions covered everything they wanted to say. Size, colour, shape, texture of skin, distance away, time of day, quality of light, everything. They felt strangely satisfied after the questions, at least their experience had now been recorded, though not officially, and this very pleasant, sympathetic and experienced man, believed them.

Armstrong wanted to find out more, as much as he could. He was even more convinced now that they would stay here on Loch Ness for an indefinite period, even for a few years. He was excited, wanting to dedicate himself to hunting the creature.

'How come nobody's managed to get a really good shot after all these years?' she asked.

Bell smiled. 'It's mainly the distance problem, the chances are that from most vantage points the creature will appear at a distance of a considerable amount of yards, the loch is so vast. The other problem is the suddenness of appearances. By the time you get over the surprise and shock of seeing it for the first time, it's already submerging again. The chances are slim for getting the camera to your eye, making a light reading and focusing, then shooting a reasonable picture. And the chances are you'll have an ordinary lens on when you're needing a telephoto. So, we continue to have all the fuzzy, out-of-focus pictures you see around you.'

They both nodded intently.

'Take your sighting yesterday. I bet even if you had a camera in your hand, even with the right lens and reading, you would still have stood and gawped.'

'Too right, we did more than just stand and gawp, we both

nearly shit ourselves.'

'You planning to hang around? Most people get the urge for monster hunting after a really good sighting.'

'Yeah,' Jack said, glancing at Tina, 'we're definitely thinking about it. We're camping on the other side of the water. We were just holidaying, you know, fishing and generally exploring the highlands. Then we saw it, don't think either of us have gotten over it yet. I was thinking, we could invest in some decent cameras and binoculars and really get into it properly.' He knew what kind of effect his words had started to have on her. She nudged him.

'Hey, hey… hang about a minute,' she was smiling, slightly falsely, colour flaring on her cheeks, 'I think we've got a lot to talk about after we leave Mr. Bell.'

'Oh, oh,' Bell said, shifting uneasily in his chair, 'I think you've got some ducking and diving to do when she gets you alone.'

Armstrong laughed and put his arm around her. 'No, I've just got a little gentle persuasion to do.' He said, kissing her on her burning cheek.

'By the way,' Bell interrupted, 'this may help you decide… have you heard about the reward?'

'No,' Jack said, 'Tell us.'

'Well… a newspaper has offered an official reward to the first person to come up with undisputed proof that some species, other than normal, inhabits the loch. An excellent photograph will do.'

'How much?' Tina asked.

'£10,000!'

Armstrong let a long slow whistle escape through his teeth.

The caravan started filling up with people.

'Looks like we've got a coach party, sorry I'll have to leave you.' Bell stood up. 'Very pleased to have met you both.' They shook hands.

'Tell you what, have you got anything planned for this afternoon?' he asked.

'No, nothing.' Jack answered.

'Right. Do you know the Culloden Arms?'

'No, but we'll find it.' Jack said.

'It's in Drumnadrochit, just down the road. Ask anyone in the village. I'm always in there at lunchtime. It's my afternoon off today, I'd like to take you to meet someone. He could really help you if you're serious about it.'

'We're serious alright, see you there.'

'Right, about oneish then.'

'Bye Mr. Bell,' she said as Jimmy Bell walked across to greet the tourists.

She walked ahead towards the car in silence, and he knew she was upset. He knew he would have to watch what he said for the moment. There was no way she was going to be bulldozed away from her dream of married life in Cornwall. He'd have to be subtle, gradually ease her towards his thinking. Loch Ness had got to him. He knew he was already trapped in its mysterious grip.

'Hey, come on babe,' he said gently holding her arm just as she was about to get into the car. She spun round on him. 'You selfish bastard.' He drew back, the words slapping him in the face.

'For God's sake, what's up with you?' he stammered.

'You know fucking well what's up!' The gutter language

spewing from her mouth for the first time since Aberdeen.

'If you decide to stay here and go chasing the fucking monster, it'll mean you've got me here on false pretences. I came away with you because I thought we were going to get married and settle down. Now you're talking about chasing round here for the next... God knows how long... where do you think that leaves me?' The tears welled up in her eyes, she turned away from him.

He grabbed her by the shoulders and spun her round to face him again, her words making his temples pound. 'Here you fucking go again... false pretences, for shit sake. You're always on about fucking giving up that lousy life you were leading as if it was some great sacrifice. Well go back then, I'm not stopping you... go back and kill yourself... go back to wallowing in all that booze and filth. You know...,' he had to say it, 'you know what I think your trouble is...' She struggled free from his grasp and strode off to the edge of the cliff. She knew from experience what was coming next. He shouted after her. 'The trouble with you is you're not getting enough... of it all... one man just isn't enough for you!'

She had found the top of some steps leading down the steep hillside and had disappeared down them. Suddenly he was calmer. He'd said what he was bursting to say. He'd slashed back and hurt. Now the pent-up feelings had climaxed he slumped back against the side of the car. There was silence again, except for a lark singing high over the cliff edge. He looked across the car park at the caravans.

The tail end of the coach party was still queuing outside the main caravan and they were all looking across at him.

'Oh, bollocks to the lot of you...' he muttered and walked

over to the steps.

She was sitting about a dozen steps down, her knees drawn up under her chin, looking down the loch. He walked down and sat beside her.

'Before you start your apologies, don't, I can't bear going over all that old ground over and over again, I know you're feeling sorry for yourself, and I know I am too.' She said.

'I shouldn't have gone off the way I did.'

He put his arm around her. 'I love you.'

'Yeah,' she said softly.

They climbed down the narrow rock steps that twisted down the steep hillside through the fern covered rocks and clumps of heather down to the foreshore where they spent the rest of the morning.

'Just look at that water,' he said, 'not even a ripple.'

He picked up a pebble and lobbed it in.

'If it surfaced now, what a fantastic shot we could have. We must buy a decent camera and lenses.'

She held out her hand to him. 'Look, I've been thinking… the way things are between us at the moment, maybe it would be better if we stall things for a while.'

They sat down on a boulder under an overhanging willow at the base of the cliff face. She gripped his hand tightly.

'Up till now I've wanted nothing else but to get down to Cornwall and get married. But suddenly I don't want that anymore… not with the way you've been recently.' He sat looking out across the loch, his eyes adjusting to the distance, the familiar forms of their tent and the campsite coming into focus on the far side.

She continued, 'you want to stay… so we'll stay. Maybe we

need the time to see what will happen, I mean between us.'

'And what will you do if things don't work out for us?'

She sighed, her eyes filling with tears, 'I don't know.'

He put his arm around her and drew her to him turning her head to face his. Gently he kissed her wet eyelids. 'I love you, Teen. I want to go to Cornwall. I want to marry you. It's just…' She put her fingers over his lips. 'Sssh… I know, we'll give it a whirl here for a while, and by the way, I love you too,' she kissed him, 'and maybe we can learn to love that bloody monster as well.'

'Trust me, Teen. This is going to be a lovely adventure, then we head for Cornwall.'

He picked up a smooth flat pebble and skimmed it low over the water. It skipped once, twice, three times before disappearing, leaving three sets of circular ripples that spread into each other and melted again into the glass-like surface.

'What a fantastic day,' he said, 'a perfect day for another sighting.'

CHAPTER THREE

The Culloden Arms was a small grey two storey stone building that vaguely resembled a castle. It had some turreting along the roof parapets, gothic shaped windows and front door. An old swinging inn sign hung above the front door. The sign depicted a scene from the Battle of Culloden, that horrific confrontation in which the highland clans were butchered by the English only a few short miles away on bleak Culloden Moor. They pushed open the heavy oak door and stepped inside to a comfortable interior smelling of furniture polish, and good cooking. The ceiling was low and beamed and hung with hundreds of pewter tankards. The walls were lined with clan tartans and flags of every kind, and oil paintings, prints and writings, all connected with the battle. Above the bar were crossed claymores over a targ. The furniture was dark and heavy in the Jacobean style.

'Nice,' she said.

'Bit touristy.' He murmured.

There were about fifteen people in the bar, with plenty of day-glo anoraks in evidence. Jimmy Bell was sitting on a bar stool at the end of the bar. He waved to them as they entered.

'Hi,' he greeted, 'nice to see you again, what's your poison?'

'I'll have a pint of Youngers,' Jack replied.

'And what about you… err Tina, sorry I'm terrible with names, 'Tina and Jack, right.'

'Whew… half a cold lager thanks,' she smiled. 'it's already

getting hot out there.'

Halves of lager where her only drink these days. Somehow, she hadn't felt the need for anything harder since she had left Aberdeen. She had convinced herself that her problem must only have been a social one, due entirely to the hopeless environment she'd lived in and the company she kept. The bouts of amnesia, however, would always haunt her… she had no illusions about them. It sickened her to think of those days.

'Pull up a couple of stools, what you been doing since I last saw you?'

'Oh, we just took a walk along the shore below the Bureau. The water's beautiful today, a really flat calm.'

'Typical weather today,' Bell said. 'most sightings are made on days like today, you know, hot, hazy, flat calm.'

'Really, why's that do you think?' Tina asked.

'My theory is that the creature likes basking, same as whales or other large fish. As soon as the sun's warm enough and the surface is free from waves, up they come and just laze about. People have observed them for quite long periods like that, humps out of the water. They're often mistaken for upturned boats.'

'Until they rear their ugly heads!' She said, giving a mock shudder.

'We've talked about it and have definitely decided to stay for a while,' he said. 'we're going to invest in some decent cameras and binoculars.'

'Good,' Bell said, 'there'll be lots of disappointments and life will be tough at times, but you'll enjoy it.'

'I guess so,' she said, a little glumly.

'Remember the weather isn't always going to be like this.

You've got to get through a highland winter under canvas before you'll really know all about it. That can be anything but fun.' Bell said, paying the barman.

Armstrong took a big swig from his jug. 'We'd be grateful for any help and advice you can give us and, of course, we will always be available to give you a hand at the Bureau if ever you need it.'

'Thanks, I'll take you up on that.' Bell said.

'Anyway, who is this person you want us to meet?'

'Right,' Bell settled himself on his stool, leaning back against the corner wall, elbow on the bar. 'This guy is probably the best expert on the Loch Ness phenomenon there is. He has lived by the loch for seven years, camping on the bank. He's had hundreds of sightings and has photographed the creature umpteen times. Many of the photographs in my exhibition have been taken by him.'

'You mean even he hasn't had as good a sighting as us?' Jack said.

'No, he's had some darned good ones, but nothing like you've described.'

'That makes my heart sink,' said Tina, 'to think we could hang around for the next seven years and…'

'No,' Bell interrupted. 'you just wait till you meet this man, see some of his pictures, listen to some of his stories… he'll really get you going.'

'Who is he?' Jack asked, 'and why is he doing it?'

'They call him Red Angus,' Bell said, 'but be warned, the man's a great big gentle giant when he's happy, but he's dangerous when roused or drunk, and he's both those often enough. He hits the whisky with a vengeance, some say to forget some personal tragedy from way back, they said he had a wife and kiddie once. He was with the Argyll and Sutherland Highlanders, joined up when this family tragedy, whatever it was, struck. Then went A.W.O.L. and became a mercenary, was in the Congo during its bloodbath. From what I hear, most of the blood was spilled by him. A kind of vengeance against a world that had shown him no mercy.'

'Well, one thing's for sure, he's not going to be a bore.' She said.

They followed Bell's land-rover for about ten minutes before it turned off the road and down a dirt track that ended at a rough lichen covered dry stone wall and stile. On the other side of the wall the hill dropped away suddenly for approximately 300 feet to the loch below.

'How the hell do we get down there?' Jack asked as Bell climbed over the stile.

'There are stone steps on the other side of that clump of boulders,' Bell said, 'it's quite safe but be careful.'

Jack helped Tina over, then climbed over himself. They followed Bell diagonally down and across the spongy turf to the clump of boulders. The steps were man made, but narrow and steep. They dropped almost straight down for about 50 feet, then turned and disappeared behind rocks and gorse.

Tina's head spun as she gazed down, feeling invisible hands pushing her from behind.

'Shit… can I be last, otherwise I think I'll be breaking the high dive record.'

'Don't look down to the loch, just look at your feet.' Bell warned.

'I'm just glad it's not raining or windy,' Jack laughed, 'come on Teen, stick behind me.'

'No good sticking behind you if you fall... be careful.' She pleaded.

Five minutes later they arrived at another stone wall that seemed to cut upwards diagonally almost from the water's edge. Bell pointed down to a kind of inlet with a narrow beach of shingle and rocks at the mouth of a stream with sheer cliffs hanging over on both sides, forming a tiny natural harbour. They could see a tent, looking more like a postage stamp from that height and a small boat tied to a jetty.

'That's his house,' Bell said, 'hope he's in, I don't fancy the thought of clambering about these cliffs in vain.'

'Jees... you mean he has to climb up and down here every time he has to go somewhere?' she said.

'He doesn't go anywhere, except occasionally into Aberdeen when he needs a binge.' Bell said. 'He's a strange one is big Red, bit of a recluse really, he fishes and hunts and grows his own vegetables, doesn't want for a thing. He keeps a big old motorbike on the road, which he bombs about the moors on when the mood takes him. Otherwise he boats up to a suitable landing stage if he needs to go anywhere.'

They jumped down onto a narrow strip of pebbles, on the opposite side of the stream from the campsite.

'Don't get your feet wet.' Bell said as he tip-toed over on a row of flat stepping stones.

'There he is.' Bell pointed.

They saw a man kneeling at the water's edge pulling in a hand line.

'Afternoon Red.' Bell shouted.

The man didn't turn around but greeted back. 'Afternoon Jimmy boy. Come on the scrounge again I suppose. Me and Tiger have just shared a lovely little baked trout, so hard fucking luck!' He chuckled hoarsely, but still didn't turn around.

Bell laughed. 'Come now Red, mind your language, you've got visitors and one's a lady.'

The man stopped hauling in the line and turned suddenly and stood up.

'Och, I'm sorry.'

He stood over six feet tall and must have weighed fifteen stone. Dark red curly hair and a beard framed a ruggedly handsome face, tanned and weathered by years of sun and harsh highland winters. It was a hard, tough face, but the lines that creased the corners of his sky-blue eyes when he smiled betrayed a joviality that softened the look of the man.

A big khaki slouch hat reminiscent of Australia or the African bush was pushed back on the flaming curls. He was stripped to the waist, displaying a near perfect torso, honed to hard fitness by the life he led, and was still leading. His skin had a sheen of perspiration adding and accentuating the muscles moving under the deeply tanned skin. On his chest, marring the near perfection, was an enormous purple and red tattoo of a thistle.

Bell had said this man was fifty but looking at him standing there they would have guessed he was in his late thirties. They couldn't help but stare at the rest of his garb. A tartan kilt, leather sporran, and heavy army ammunition boots.

He strode up beaming 'Morning,' grasping Jack's hand. The grip was vice-like.

Then, 'and you my dear…' instantly she noticed the change

41

in his expression. An almost imperceptible look. The smiling eyes suddenly widening, the broad grin freezing for an instant as his lips parted then tightened again in silent shock. Her blood raced, she'd caught the split-second reaction... he'd recognised her. This stranger knew her.

Oh God, had Jack noticed... this is all they needed. She flicked a glance at Jack, he was looking at Red Angus and she thought she could see a reddening in his cheeks, a sudden tenseness in his face.

'Hello me dear,' Red Angus grunted, taking her hand gently, the words growling up from deep down in the barrel chest somewhere.

Bell spoke, 'I brought these two friends of mine along to meet you Red. They've decided to stay on the loch for a while.'

Red Angus laughed, 'Aha... and what wee thing has made them do that I'm wondering?'

'They've had the best sighting of us all, that's why.' Bell said.

The big Scotsman looked serious. 'Aye, now you're talking, wait a minute while I haul in my eel line, then I'll get you a couple of stiff slugs of what the highlands are made of.

They watched him put on some heavy leather gloves and start pulling in the line. It was of thick orange two-ply nylon, the end of which was tethered to a thick stake hammered into the water's edge.

'Whatever you have on there seems pretty heavy.' Jack ventured. She noticed that Jack had regained his relaxed mood and wondered again if he really had noticed that flicker of surprise in Red Angus's face, and the desperate blush on her own. Her heart thumped as she wondered where she could have met this man... when? In what circumstance? She would have had to be drunk… filthy, stinking, pissed in some Aberdeen alleyway. Oh God, like a randy alley cat. He was a very striking looking man, not the kind of man to forget easily. Her mind conjured up depraved images in her paranoia and the thoughts brought feelings of nausea welling up in the pit of her stomach.

'You ok love?' Jack stepped over to her side and put his arm round her shoulder, 'You look like death.'

He was behaving so normally, he couldn't know. The feelings began to ebb as quickly as they had come, she shrank into him, sliding her arm round his waist.

'I'm ok darling… must have been that hike down the hillside.' She smiled up at him.

'They'll be heavy alright,' Red Angus said. 'This line goes down about a hundred feet, there are some big old devils down there.'

Soon a baited hook appeared at the surface. It was tied to the main line by a foot-long length of finer nylon. Then another and another, at regular three-yard intervals. The hooks were baited with big strips of whitish substance.

'What's your bait?' Jack asked. 'Rabbit liver.' Red grunted, as they suddenly glimpsed the eel, spiralling to the surface. Its pale underside looking yellow in the peaty water. Then it was on the bank writhing into its own coils, the nylon line tangled and cutting into its flesh. It was coughing a red mucus through its clenched jaws, so tightly clamped onto the hook that the big barbs had pierced the roof of its mouth and were protruding through one of its eyes. Red picked up a butcher's knife, stood on the squirming body with his left boot and sawed its head off. The headless coils bled and squirmed away on the pebbles, while he hauled in another and then another, beheading each in turn. Soon the lead weight came in at the end of the line.

'Four fat beauties.' Red chuckled.

They were all around three feet long and thick as a big man's wrist.

Any of these eels would have made an ordinary fisherman somewhere else in the country very happy indeed, Jack thought.

'What will you do with them?' Tina asked. Red looked down at the writhing bodies and grinned.

'Well, I think I'll be putting one away for frying tonight, and I'll smoke the others for later, you ever had smoked eel?'

She grimaced, 'no.'

'Delicious, nothing like it, especially with home-baked bread.' Red muttered, making even those revolting things on the blood-splattered pebbles sound desirable. He set about pulling the severed heads off the hooks. 'Good bait... for eels,' he said, laughing loudly.

Soon they were all sitting down round a camp table outside the tent. Red produced a bottle of Glenfiddich and proceeded to pour out huge slugs.

'Oh, please, only a small one for me.' She tried to protest. 'You trying to give up?' the question caught her unawares. She glanced up at the Scotsman and caught the twinkle in his eye.

'Och... come on,' he rasped, and poured, she squirmed, 'any chance of some ginger?'

'What!' Red bellowed. 'You canna mix a beautiful malt whisky like this with anything, come on, sip it gently, this is no ordinary scotch.'

She sipped, noticing the different taste, but not particularly liking it.

'Right,' said Red Angus, settling down with at least four fingers of Glenfiddich. 'So you've seen the wee monster have you? Tell me all about it.'

Jack started from the beginning, and Red Angus sat, serious and silent, listening intently, breaking in occasionally to go over some detail.

'Well, if you're telling me the truth, and I canna see why you should lie, then I'm very envious. I wish I'd had your sighting, I've been here all these years and never seen anything as good.'

'Jimmy tells us you've taken many photographs, can we see them?' Jack asked.

Bell stood up. 'Look, I think I'd better get going. I have a few things to do in Inverness this afternoon, so I'll leave you with Red and hope to see you soon. Thanks for the drink Red.'

Jack and Tina stood up, they shook hands and thanked him.

'We'll drop in on you as soon as we've settled, thanks again.' Jack said. Bell started on the long climb up the hill to his land-rover.

'Right,' Red poured out two more Glenfiddichs for Jack and himself. Tina's whisky level hadn't altered. 'Where were we… yes, your sighting. What did you do about it?'

'I telephoned the *Inverness Echo* and the *Highland Tribune*, but they virtually laughed at me. Besides that, we went to Jimmy Bell, and now we're with you. That's about it.'

'If you had got a decent shot at that range, you'd have caused a sensation laddie and made a bit of money. But there you go, taking the right picture is the hardest thing of all.'

'Yes, I can see that.' Jack agreed.

'Yeah,' Red grunted, 'cameras and photographs have a strange habit of jamming and fogging at the crucial moment.

A very famous monster hunter, Tim Corbett, who took the best cine film of all time and had written and published a couple of best sellers on the creature, missed a perfect opportunity a year or so ago. The creature's head and neck appeared in front of him at about a hundred yards, in conditions as clear as a bell. Do you know what happened? After months of concentrated watching, he was temporarily paralysed with shock and excitement and failed to activate any of the telephoto cameras that he had ready.'

'Goodness, he must have felt like drowning himself!' Tina laughed.

'Here's another story,' Red continued. 'another famous monster photographer, who had a lot of photographs published, managed at last to get a really good series of shots of a first-class sighting. That's when his trouble started. First his main batch of colour slides went on the missing list at the local newspaper offices, I think it was. Then, a second set went missing in the post on the way to the Academy of Applied Sciences in Boston, Massachusetts. Then finally, his last good shot, which was an original glass negative, copied from one of the best of the missing bunch, was accidently dropped and broken… by the photographer himself.'

'Wow!' Jack exclaimed.

'Goodness, we just don't know what it's all about yet,' Tina glumly said.

'No, you must never think like that,' Red urged. 'the one thing you've just got to have is patience here on the loch.' He knocked back his drink and poured another full glass for himself. 'I've had a few of my pictures published, and have made a bit of money, but it's still only a piss in the ocean. I'm still working for the big one, a shot of something like you've seen, then we're talking about real money and all the spin-offs from that, magazine articles, one's own book or two perhaps, even TV interviews. It's not the money though, I just need pennies to live from day to day. It's the wee creature, that's what I want.'

'Just how much watching do you do?' Jack asked.

'I set myself special watches every day and stick to them. It's very easy to slip into disorganisation and laziness, one has to live according to certain standards. I'm a great believer in discipline you know, personal cleanliness, daily routines. Without discipline I'd wreck my life out here.'

'Did it take a lot of getting used to, I mean when you first started?' Tina asked.

'No, not for me. After fifteen years as a pro soldier, ten of those in the regular army, the rest as a mercenary, I learned to survive or die. Aden, Malaya and the Congo. I've seen death many times. It teaches you about life, how to live. Death can be beautiful, and at the same time obscene, ugly, but you need to see its many faces before you can learn to sort yourself out, get your values organised. I can't bear to see the slow death of our society in the so-called modern world... the swinging sixties, ugh! We're destroying ourselves, that's why I'm so fascinated with the mystery of the loch. A completely untouched species! Those years prepared me for what I'm doing now. You'll need strength many times from now on, mental as well as physical, and you'll need the strength of each other.' He suddenly laughed. 'Don't look so bloody worried. Och, you should see your faces!'

They both smiled. 'You haven't told us what your theory is,

what the creature is.' Tina said.

'Theory? I know what it is. Nobody else agrees with me, but I know.'

'Plesiosaur.' Jack said.

He laughed loudly again. 'Do you mean to say you still don't know after a close-up sighting like that?'

'What then?' Tina asked. 'We saw a close up of a dozen different parts of something's anatomy.'

'Giant eel.' Red tipped back the last of his glass and banged it empty onto the camp table-top, then poured another.

'Eel?' they both exclaimed in unison.

'Yeah, a bloody great eel. No ordinary eel mind… you know the moray?'

'Moray?' Jack almost choked on his drink, but that's strictly a marine fish.'

'Yes, but I'm talking about a hybrid of some kind, not the moray we know. This glen became landlocked from the sea millions of years ago, a primeval earthquake.'

'I know morays, came across them a lot in the Gulf of Mexico… evil bastards,' said Armstrong, almost shuddering.

'Well imagine something five times the size of the biggest moray in the sea.'

'You're joking. This goes against anything anybody else believes,' Jack said. 'Besides, a monster like that would be a rampaging killer, and we all know the Loch Ness monster doesn't kill.'

'It does,' Red Angus shrugged, 'not people, because people don't give it a chance. People just don't venture out onto the loch to any great extent. Do you know, I've seen a big stag being taken? Deer regularly swim across the loch, and deer regularly end up as eel fodder.'

'Jeez, this is mind blowing,' Jack said. 'you mean this creature is a throwback, a prehistoric equivalent to the common moray of our modern seas?'

'Yes, the species would have been trapped when the ends of the loch became sealed off during the immense upheaval in pre-history and has survived to breed and thrive because it wasn't subject to the changes that eventually made the species extinct. Simply because it has been protected from its natural environment, with no natural enemies… not yet anyway.'

'Ok,' Jack said, 'what about all those head and neck shots and all the sightings. Surely all that's much more Plesiosaur than giant eel.'

'You obviously don't know eels.'

They both looked puzzled.

He continued, 'eels can control their bodies just like snakes. If one is observant enough, wherever there is water… marshes, canals or stagnant margins, anywhere that eels abound, it's often possible to see them raise their heads and half their bodies to almost vertical, either out of the water or off the bottom to snatch prey from the water surface. They're excellent cobra impersonators.'

'For shit sake then,' Jack said, 'why on earth is the scientific world so reticent about this whole Loch Ness thing, be it Plesiosaur, giant eel or myth?'

'The attitude of the so-called scientific world laddie,' Red stabbed a finger at Jack 'is that if you haven't got a carcass to dissect in a laboratory, then it ain't worth considering.'

'It's criminal.' Tina ventured.

'Yeah,' Red muttered, 'it's bloody frustrating at times. The whole damn world treats the monster as a joke instead of what it really represents… a major zoological discovery in a world in which nature itself is becoming extinct. Yeah, there are times I've become disenchanted enough to join the hunt for Charlie's Gold.'

'Charlie's Gold?' Jack asked.

'You mean you've never heard of Charlie's Gold?'

'No, we haven't.'

He laughed loudly. 'Hell, there's a lot you two have still to learn about Loch Ness.'

'Tell.' Tina demanded.

'Well, legend has it that when Bonnie Prince Charlie came over from France to lead us highland Scots against the English, he came with a small fortune in French gold coin. Money that would see him to the throne of England. Well, we all know what happened, the Scots were thrashed at Culloden Moor only a few miles from where we're sitting. The highland clans were practically wiped out by the Duke of Cumberland's murderers, Charlie Stuart did a bunk via the Isle of Skye and Charlie's Gold did a vanishing act as well.'

'The gold went with him?' Jack asked.

'No, the retreat was a complete shambles. There was utter chaos, with the English Redcoats riding down and butchering everything in a kilt, including women and wee bairns. Somewhere amid the slaughter the gold went missing. One thing is certain though, the treasure that was supposed to have been the passport to the throne for the Bonnie Prince wasn't with him during his escape over the sea to Skye. There is much evidence that it was still around these mountains and moors for weeks after the battle. There are legends, some of them true, some just myths, of intrigue and murder surrounding the fortune. Many are supposed to have died in the struggle for the gold.'

'What happened to it in the end?' Tina asked wide eyed.

'If I knew that, I'd be a rich man, not that I'm interested, you can keep material riches, no good to me. Give me a twelve bore, a fishing rod, a boat and some canvas over my head anytime. They say the gold is buried somewhere around the loch.'

'You mean at the bottom?'

'Yes, there's an old tale about a couple of fleeing clansmen being spotted rowing across the loch with the treasure in their boat. They were fired upon by some Redcoats and they and Charlie's Gold went to the bottom.'

'Are there many people searching for it?'

'Oh, there's always a number. Many, usually tourists and enthusiastic amateurs get the bug for a while, then lose interest and drop out, but there is a handful of really dedicated treasure hunters who have been searching for a very long time. A few of them will stop at nothing to get their hands on it.'

'I can't say I'd mind digging up a pot of Jacobite gold.' Jack sighed.

The sun had gradually crept from behind a rocky formation high above them and suddenly the little cove was washed with its warm rays.

'Look, it's a grand afternoon, how would you like me to take you out in the boat? It's a great day for a sighting, monsters love this weather.'

'Oh great, fantastic.' They both jumped at the offer.

An hour later found them in mid-Loch and for the first time

they experienced the feeling of Loch Ness. Its enormous size, the incredible feeling of isolation on its vast flat surface, and the overpowering presence of the bleak mountains and high moors on all sides.

Red Angus had cut the outboard and the silence was immense.

'The loch can be frightening, can't it?' Red smiled.

'Yeah, it can.' Tina shuddered.

'Just think of the depths below us.' Jack said.

'Yes, we're afloat on about 700 feet of water at this spot, that's about twice the height of St. Paul's Cathedral.' Red muttered. He started the motor again.

'That's a welcome sound right now,' she said, 'very comforting.'

Red laughed hoarsely. 'Don't worry, you'll get used to the loch, it has many moods, you'll have to learn to know them. We'll chug slowly down the middle as far as Cherry Island, then head back along the bank to camp. You never know, we may see something.'

Nothing much happened on the way to the island. They had been chugging slowly back for about five minutes when a shoal of small trout suddenly shot out of the water and skittered in a wide fan over the surface.

'What made them do that?' Tina exclaimed, looking anxious.

'Most likely pike, or maybe salmon,' Red said, 'although I've seen that happen on a couple of occasions before a sighting.' He cut the motor, and complete silence fell on them again, except for a faint car horn somewhere up on the Foyers Road. She moved along the seat against Jack, he put his arm around her. They watched Red, he sat there, eyes moving back and forth over the area where the trout had leapt. He reached for a paddle, watched again in silence for a few seconds, then dipped the paddle into the water and gently glided the boat forward, watching all the time. After five minutes they'd covered most of the area. He put the paddle down and carefully stood up looking into the water.

'There,' he suddenly whispered, 'look there, but be careful, stand up very carefully.'

'Shit, what is it?' Jack whispered, 'don't tell me…'

'No, it ain't the bloody monster, just shut up and take a look boy.'

They stood up holding each other. 'There now, over there, can you see him?' They followed the line of his pointed finger and there it was, lying a couple of feet below the surface, a massive pike.

'God, he must be at least four feet long.' Jack hissed.

The fish lay there, stiff like a log, it's disguise complete except for the gently moving tail.

'He missed his dinner that time,' Red smiled, 'let's see if we can tempt him to have another bash.' He knelt down in the bottom of the boat and carefully reached under the stern planking.

'Very quiet now, no movement.' He warned, extricating a small stout spinning rod all set up ready for use. They watched as he stood up very slowly, a huge yellow lure at the end of the line.

'Wow,' Jack whispered, 'that's some plug.' It must have been a foot long with four sets of hooks hanging from it. It was crudely painted yellow with black stripes, and two big black and white eyes.

'Made it myself,' the Scot hissed, 'no ordinary tackle will do on Loch Ness.'

'What you aiming to do with that thing, frighten the pike to death?' Jack smiled.

Red turned and glared at him, then he opened the bale arm, steadied himself and cast skilfully, allowing the lure to fall about five yards past the fish. He started to retrieve, the pike hadn't moved. The lure dived, and they watched breathless as it cavorted, weaving enticingly towards the pike as Red guided it, twitching the tip to improve its performance. He manoeuvred it to within a foot of the pike's head and slid past the great jaws without a flicker of response from the fish. He reeled in, the fish remained frozen, still masquerading as a half sunken log. He cast again, the lure hit the same spot on the water.

'Come on, me beauty, take a bite of cold steel,' he hissed.

Suddenly an almost invisible movement in the pike, a flicker of awareness,

'Yes,' Red twitched the rod tip, 'he's decided to take.'

The big tail flicked, propelling the fish into a blinding open jawed, head on collision with the four big hooks and painted wood. Too late to back off, the hooks entangled in its jaws. It shook its big head from side to side, turning away from them, its body arched like a bow, jaws and gills distorted with sideways strain from the line. Red steadied himself as the boat rocked then listed over towards the fish. He stood leaning back, knees bent and legs apart. The rod bent almost double as he applied pressure, then suddenly straightened as the line went slack.

'He's heading towards us.' Red grunted, and wound in the slack as fast as he could so as to keep a tight line. They saw the fish heading towards them just below the surface. They could see its eyes, they seemed to be looking at them. It passed under the boat, pulling the rod tip down with it, tilting the boat even further. Tina whimpered, gripping the gunnels with white knuckled terror.

'God, it's going to pull us with it.'

'It's ok baby, just hang on.' Jack gripped her around the waist. She wondered how scared he was.

Red turned, manoeuvring the rod round so that the line passed over the stern and freed itself. The pike was swimming downwards fast, stripping the line from the reel. He tightened the drag to give more resistance, but the clutch screeched on as the pike bored down into the blackness of the deep, stopping again and again to twist and roll and shake its great head, then continue to dive deeper, to swim as far away as possible from its tormentors, to find refuge somewhere in the dark, to rest.

'Running out of line fast,' Red shouted, 'gotta apply some pressure, bring him up again.'

He started to pump the rod. This meant heaving upwards, then reeling in the slack line, then repeating the action again and again in a pump action, the rod butt deep in his groin, both hands working the rod, the muscles bulging and moving on his arms. Tina watched him fascinated, her eyes taking him in, mesmerised by the power of the man. She became aware of a sensation deep inside as her gaze lingered on the bent legs, as his kilt rode high on his thighs. What was this incredible man to her, what experience had she shared with him?

'I think it's tiring,' he gasped. Gradually the reel was filling with line again, but every few seconds it would scream as the pike realised it was losing the battle and turned to make a run again. Jack and Tina looked in the water, they couldn't see anything in the blackness, just the line hissing across the surface. Suddenly the line was slack again.

'Here we go, he's coming out of the water.'

They saw the fish suddenly take on a new lease of life, but instead of running away it was rocketing upwards. It broke surface about ten yards from the boat, shuddering into the air, shaking its head, then crashing down again, then up again. It seemed to walk along the surface on its tail for a few seconds, then flop down and disappear.

'That's its lot, shot its bolt now, what do you think of that circus act?' Red laughed.

'Shit, I've never seen anything like it.' Jack shouted in high pitched excitement.

'Yeah, these loch pike are a very different kettle of fish.' He laughed at his own pun. They laughed and wondered how often he'd used it in the past.

The rod was still bucking, and the line still taut.

'I'll give him a few more minutes to swim around, he's nearly finished now.' Red said sitting down. Still holding the rod with both hands, the butt under his arm, he motioned to Tina.

'There's a wee flask in my sporran,' and he gestured with his eyes. She looked down at his open legs at the leather sporran and felt her face flush, then glanced at Jack. She bent down, opened the flap and eased out the whisky flask, her heart thumping with embarrassment.

The bastard, she thought, the bastard.

'Would you like a wee dram to calm your nerves?' She could see the twinkle in his eye.

She shook her head.

'No.' Jack said.

She could see he was plainly angry.

You're going to have to train her laddie,' Red chuckled. 'nothing wrong with a wee dram now and again,' he winked at her knowingly.

'Where's the gaff?' Jack broke in flushed and irritated.

Red laughed. 'Haven't used a gaff in ten years.'

She was sure the big Scotsman was goading them and belittling Jack. She was angry enough to push the big bastard overboard, scared too. Scared by her own feelings.

'Ok, let's see how you do it then.' Jack said, feeling the anger thumping in his chest. There were vague fears building inside him, feelings he couldn't put his finger on. Red continued to play the fish. There was hardly any fight left now. The rod tremored occasionally, and the line was slicing to and fro across the surface.

Jack looked at his watch. It was a full ten minutes since the pike first attacked the lure, ten minutes that had flashed by like a second.

They could see the pike swimming slowly, but still pulling back every time Red forced it too near the boat.

'Alright my beauty, I've got plenty of time.' It turned on its side then righted itself again. Red reeled in, the fish was alongside now, he transferred the rod to his left hand, keeping the rod tip up. They watched him, wondering what he'd do next.

'Watch this me darlings,' he said, 'a thirty pound plus loch pike landed without net or gaff.' He reached over the side with his right arm, gently felt under the great lower jaw, found the soft niche he wanted, waited a second or two, the pike lay still, a spent force at his mercy, then he deftly and in one smooth movement lifted the fish onto the boat. It lay there, jaws moving, tail flapping gently on the planking.

'That'll teach you to go after painted ladies, won't it,' Red whispered, 'now let's see if we can get those hooks out without too much pain.' They noticed a gentleness in his voice now as they watched him carefully easing the cruel barbs from the mouth.

'We'll soon have you back in the water my beauty.'

Tina watched him with fascination, this big rough highlander who looked capable of brute violence, then in an instant this display of tenderness.

They arrived back at Red Angus's cove at about six o'clock.

A wind had been gradually building up, now it was strong and whipping the loch surface into waves a foot high.

'Incredible how quickly the wind can build up.' Jack said as they helped Red pull the boat up onto the shingle under the cliff.

'Yes, you wouldn't credit it. It can change in minutes from a flat calm to gale force. The Great Glen forms a natural wind tunnel from the North to South. I've seen waves to nigh on eight feet whipped up in minutes. It can be as dangerous as the open sea, and no joke to be caught out unprepared.

He tied the boat up and covered it. 'Well, I don't know about you people but I'm starving, why don't you stay for supper?'

The hours in the open air out on the loch had sharpened their appetites. 'We're ravenous,' Tina said.

'Ok then, I'll fix you one of my specialities, rabbit casserole.'

'Sounds great,' Jack said, 'Im so hungry I could eat the monster without waiting to cook it!'

'Shot a nice buck this morning. I've already skinned and

gutted him, so supper won't be long.' He walked over to a small canvas lean-to built into the cliff wall. A large food cabinet with a fine wire mesh front, stood with its legs in four big flat bottom salmon tins. Jack noticed these and remembered seeing the same kind of thing in the tropics. The tins were filled with paraffin or oil to prevent insects or other creepy crawlies getting at the food. Red took a big carcass from the cabinet. 'You ever used a pressure cooker my darling?' he looked at Tina.

'No, never been one for any fancy cooking,' she said and wondered if he was getting at her again.

'Well,' he growled, splaying the rabbit out on a wooden board on the table, 'number one, you've got to learn there's nothing more cheery than a good delicious meal on a bleak winter's day up here on the loch, especially when you've spent most of the day in the open and you're damp and chilled to the marrow. There's nothing that can pick up the old morale like a good hot meal. You can't live on fried stuff and out of cans, do that and it won't be more than a few days before you start feeling sorry for yourselves. One thing you can't do up here in mid-winter under canvas is feel sorry for yourselves. Real cooking needn't take long, not with a pressure cooker. You can cook a full meal, meat, vegetables, the lot in minutes, and you can do it on a tiny gas stove if need be.'

They watched as he skilfully and quickly prepared the meal. First, he sliced up two big onions. Then he heated some oil in the pressure cooker and threw in the onions with a flourish. 'Must get your seasoning right before you start cooking,' he said. He then added ground black pepper, garlic, salt and a good splurge of Soy Sauce and Worcester Sauce. Soon the little cove filled with the delicious aroma of frying onions sizzling in their seasoning.

'Mmmm.' Tina murmured.

'Yeah, I'm slavering.' Jack grinned.

Then Red tossed the pieces of rabbit he'd chopped up into the pot and stirred the mixture together.

'Now you let the lot fry for a few minutes, fill this.' He handed Tina an aluminium jug and gestured to the stream. 'That water's as pure as ever you'll get it.' He poured the water in, stirred again, then put the lid on twisting it shut and fixing the steam valve. 'Ten minutes and it'll be ready,' he said.

They sat round the table which he'd set with a bottle of Spanish red wine and another big whisky for himself.

The meal was even more delicious than it had smelled, and soon they were sitting back, their appetites satisfied, with a comfortable muzzy glow from the wine which remained only an inch high in the bottle.

'Come on, just a drop left,' he said, pouring the inch into her glass.

'Thank you, that was one of the most enjoyable meals we've had in a long time.' Jack said, lighting up a small cheroot.

'Why does food always taste so good in the open air?' she said.

'My grub tastes good anywhere,' Red Angus growled proudly, 'and you've got no excuse now you've been taught.' He drained his glass again.

'You promised to show us your photographs.'

'Yes, so I did.' He went to the tent and emerged with a big thick album. It was a white leathered one with a kind of cushioned cover on which was printed 'Our Wedding' in silver.

'Used to be my wedding album,' he said, a hint of sadness

in his gruff voice.

'Oh…' Jack started.

'Yes, I was married once… once a long time ago.'

'Ok, let's have a look at my new woman,' he laughed, opening the album, 'first, a drop of what does you good… some whisky?'

'Oh no… no thanks.' They both said.

'Alright, I'm used to drinking on my own,' he smiled. He poured himself a good five inches and knocked back a large slug.

The album was full of incredible photographs, some of which they remembered seeing blown up at Jimmy Bell's bureau. He went through and talked about each one in turn. There were many shots of head and neck shapes and many more of backs and hump-like protrudences, varying from quite close-up to distant, grainy black images on the water surface.

'This is the one that could have been the winner, if, if, if,' he said turning to a close-up shot of a violent water disturbance, with a tiny black indistinguishable shape in the midst of the turmoil. He drained his glass and poured himself another. 'Yeah, it could have made me a small fortune, or a grave, dark and watery.'

'What happened?' Jack asked.

'I was out one morning two years ago,' they noticed his voice slurring now into a low growl, 'a morning just like this morning, flat calm it was, not a breath of wind. I was crossing the loch to pick up some shotgun cartridges from a mate of mine who gets them for me on his trips into Inverness. I was halfway across, all my attention focused on a pair of mating grebes, when I was bumped. It was only a gentle bump, but solid, you know, heavy. The loch at that point is about four hundred feet deep. At first I thought it could have been a half-submerged log, but then I realised I'd have hit the log with the front of the hull first, this bump was from directly underneath. Then came the next one, this time the impact was massive. The boat lurched up into the air, and came down bow first, shipping a good deal of water and began to list badly. I hung on, and believe me, I was scared half to death.'

'Shit... I bet you were.'

'I knew then that it was the creature, nothing else could have done that to the boat. The last impact had stalled the outboard, and I was trying to start it when I felt the bottom being brushed, sort of grated by something huge. Then it happened, something enormous surfaced directly behind me. Something, some part of the animal, tail perhaps, hit the boat and damn near sunk me. In those few seconds I was only concerned with hanging on and keeping afloat. When I turned, it had just submerged, I saw something that looked like a tail disappearing. I managed to get my camera up and took this picture. As you can see... sweet FA! It took many months to get over that experience, and I'm not ashamed to admit I didn't venture onto the loch again for a month.'

'Don't blame you, I think I would have packed up and gone home after that.' Jack sighed.

'This is my home, so here I am still,' he slurred, taking another gulp of whisky.

'That tail, or whatever it was, I'll never forget it,' he shuddered, 'it was a greenish brown in colour, and the underside was pale yellowish.' He had started to slouch across the table a little. His face had become flushed and the sparkling eyes had dulled.

They both began to feel uncomfortable watching him getting

drunk before their eyes. He poured more whisky. The drinking had become compulsive, he was deliberately sending himself away into a stupor, to another world, away from them.

'The smell... the one big thing I noticed was the strong smell, a stench I've never experienced before. Very fishy, but there was something else, not just fishy, a musty kind of, maybe it only came up to break wind.' He chuckled into his glass, spilling some down his arm.

She watched him with both pity and disgust and shuddered, she imagined herself in the same condition.

'Come on, who's gonna drink with old Red Angus?' he got up and lurched towards the tent. 'I'll get some glasses and another bottle... we're gonna get pissed together.'

'No, no, thanks Red, we'll go now.' Jack said.

Red Angus turned towards them, reeling back on his heels. He was frightening her now. Not just the drunkenness, but the fear that the Glenfiddich might loosen his tongue.

'Yes, come on, let's go,' she whispered.

'Not on your life, nobody refuses to drink with Red Angus.'

They could hear him stumbling about in the tent, the clunking of bottles.

'Oh hell, we can't just leave him. Maybe we should sit another one out with him.' Jack said.

'No...' she heard the strain in her own voice. 'I don't like it, he's out of his mind,' she was pulling him, 'come on, let's go!'

They realised suddenly that there was silence now from the tent interior. They stood there for a few seconds, then peered in. he was out cold on a canvas bed, his right arm outstretched hanging on the floor still holding the empty tumbler.

'Looks like we won't be having that drink with him after

all.' Jack smiled.

'Let's go!' She pleaded, grabbing him by the arm and tugging him.

It was 11pm by the time they reached the top of the stone steps and started crossing the hillside toward the stile, where had the day gone? They looked back and down. Red Angus's camp was out of sight, but it was still light enough in the gloaming to see the white flecked waves on the loch.

They reached the car safely and were soon speeding home to their campsite on the opposite side of the water.

Both were silent for most of the journey back. She laid her head back on the rest, a vague dull pain behind her eyes. She closed them and realised for the first time the tension she had felt all afternoon, and now the relief as they drove away from Red Angus and his secrets.

The vibration of the wheels on the rough tarmac coursed through her tired limbs, and she felt thankful that they would soon be in bed, and sleep would not be far behind.

While he drove, Jack's thoughts went back to early that morning and the two characters who had intruded on him. He'd thought about them on and off during the day, but now night had come, and they were heading back to the campsite he felt a strange fear growing inside him. He wished he had mentioned them to Red Angus, maybe the big Scotsman would have known something about them, who they were, what they were doing there. He found himself wishing that the Scotsman's campsite had been nearer to theirs, and this irritated him. He was jealous of Red Angus. The man had such strength, such an overbearing physical presence, a native of the highlands, supremely confident and at home in this his own wild and rugged land.

He had learned something, but he didn't know what that something was. The man was attractive, a strong sexual magnetism that must work on any woman, even Miss Tina Dream, former Aberdeen stripper and God knows what else, need be no exception.

He forced the thoughts from his mind, but although he didn't like it, he knew he could do with the Scotsman if ever they got into any trouble. He wondered if he should mention the two ruffians to her but decided against it. No point panicking her just yet. After all, the two men had done not much more than say good morning.

He was relieved to find the tent and the rest of the campsite as they had left it. Soon they had a couple of hurricane lamps and a tilly-lamp alight, and a kettle on the stove. 'I won't have a coffee,' she yawned, 'I'm sleepy and want to stay that way.'

'Ok, I'll sit up for a while.'

He sat with a mug of creamy coffee in the warm yellow glow of the lamps, feeling secure in the pool of light and watching the winged insects fluttering in from the dusky twilight gloaming.

'Quite a character, wasn't he?' she murmured sleepily from inside the tent. 'We're lucky we've made a friend of him.'

'Yep.'

CHAPTER FOUR

By dawn, the morning had taken on the same hazy stillness of the day before. Determined to start an early watch he was out on the bank by five o'clock. For some reason there was no mist and the visibility over the loch surface was excellent. With a 35mm Practika and a 500mm lens around his neck, he settled down and started scanning the water with binoculars.

The loch was empty of boats, the only signs of life were a few geese and ducks with the occasional gull searching for food. Once again, the water surface was glass like, and every movement on or just below the surface would be easy to detect. The binoculars were also round his neck, he'd have to drop them and grab the camera with no fumbling if anything showed. He wondered how he'd react, would he be quick enough, calm enough. He didn't know what would happen if the creature burst out in front of his eyes like it did only 48 hours ago. He looked again at the spot. A few tiny fish were making circles on the surface as they tried to nip at the midges. He wondered how deep the water was under that spot and knew it must shelve violently. There were many questions... what was the creature doing there when he had cast the live-bait? Was it lurking just below the surface in comparatively shallow water, or had it been much deeper down, perhaps actually in its lair and been attracted by the vibrations of the live-bait? Was its home somewhere very near, maybe a hole or a cave in the wall of the loch only a few feet from their campsite?

He wanted to know what was under the surface, the depth, the nature of the loch wall. Were there any holes or caverns that might shelter an animal and its family? The thought had entered his head more than once before, the thought of venturing under the surface, diving with scuba tanks. After all, he was a professional diver, he'd dived in some of the most dangerous waters in the world. All his gear was packed in the boot of the beetle, all he'd need would be compressed air and access to a compressor wouldn't be a problem. There was a diving expedition working on the loch, he'd remembered Jimmy Bell saying so. It excited him, and he wanted to get going immediately.

Suddenly, a movement, something happened for a fraction of a second in the right-hand periphery of his vision. He turned and stared at the spot on the water surface, there was nothing, just the glass surface and the geese. He looked quickly around, the only gulls flying over the surface were wheeling to his left, the opposite direction. He continued to stare at the spot. Perhaps it was a diving cormorant, they stayed down for long periods. He watched half expecting to see the bird suddenly pop up.

A full two minutes went by, still nothing. He trained the binoculars on the area, but not even a ripple, then he started scanning a larger area. He tried to work out how far away from the original spot the creature would be if it had been swimming. If it had been the creature, if it hadn't been his imagination, if it hadn't been a midge flying past his right eye at a range of a mere inch or two.

He was lowering his binoculars and had just turned his head when the group of geese suddenly became agitated. He raised the glasses to his eyes in time to see the group take off along the surface, running along and flapping for take-off.

Then he saw the gigantic surge of water rushing behind them, like a submarine about to surface. Then something like a periscope, but something much bigger, thicker, glistening in the sun, rising and reaching for the nearest goose.

In a panic of squawking and flapping, all but one of the birds became airborne. One was left behind to hang for a split second, to flap and get nowhere, then disintegrate in a cloud of feathers as the evil that had come for it, took it down in a crashing dive that resounded over the loch surface. A full minute later he came out of his daze and realised with fury that he had just stood there and stared. Stared in idiotic uselessness with an expensive camera and lenses round his neck instead of at his eye.

'Teen! Tina! For heaven's sake!'

'What?' she was at the tent entrance.

'The monster, it was there, right there. It attacked and ate a goose, right in front of my fucking eyes!'

The water disturbance had melted back into the glass-like surface, she could see no sign of the dramatic scene of a few minutes earlier. Ten minutes later they were still sitting on the bank, watching and willing the creature to show itself. She was huddled against him, wrapped in a blanket, naked underneath.

'I bet it lives down there somewhere,' he said.

'Of course it lives down there, silly,' she laughed.

'No, I mean I think it lives very near here. That appearance was so near to the spot, the day before yesterday's spot. Maybe there's a cave or something down there, or maybe there's a special source of food in this area.'

He knew she wouldn't like what he was going to say next.

'There's only one way we could find out,' he said, 'going down there and taking a look-see.'

'No,' she grabbed his arm, 'no way, you're not diving, for God's sake you've got no idea what might happen! No Jack, I beg of you.'

'Look baby, we decided we would give it a chance and really go after it.'

'No, I'd rather have you in one piece, I won't let you do it.'

'Hell, I've been diving in the North Sea for I don't know how long. I'm no damn amateur you know, we decided to go all out and that's what we're gonna do. It's no good pissing about, we either carry on here or we go.'

He knew what would happen now, she'd sulk for the rest of the day.

'Hey come on, cheer up, we're in this together.' She didn't say anything, just gazed out over the water.

'Look, I'm going to do it, no matter what, okay? I want to do it and I'm gonna do it.' He stood up and walked away along the bank.

She sat there, her gaze reaching out across the loch to Urquhart Castle and the hills beyond. It was still only half past six, but the loch was already coming to life. Getting ready to offer itself and its monster legend to the tourists for another day. She could see the traffic building up on the road halfway up the hillside. Coaches, family cars, caravans. She could hear the phut, phut of a pleasure boat waking somewhere. A dog barking, and already the excited laughter of children. She gazed at the water, and a cold shiver ran through her.

She tried to imagine what was under that tranquil surface. She was angry with him and his selfishness. A feeling of isolation crept into her. Strange things were beginning to happen to her… feelings that frightened but strangely excited her. Her thoughts once again turned to Red Angus. She watched Armstrong walking slowly along the bank, still watching, binoculars at the ready. A faint feeling of guilt came over her, and she decided to walk after him, but he turned and strode briskly back.

'I think I'll take a drive up to the Bureau, I want to have a chat with Bell.'

'What, you mean on your own?' she asked.

'Yeah, you start breakfast, I'll be back in no time, I want to talk to him about the diving bit. I remember him saying there was a team of divers working somewhere on the loch, we can go see them after breakfast.'

'Okay,' she said reluctantly, 'don't be too long, I'll give you half an hour, then I'll eat for two.' He smiled and put his arm around her.

'Won't be long, promise,' he kissed her, 'don't worry, I can take care of myself.'

The sound of the beetle had just died in the distance, she was peeling off six rashers of bacon, when a snout nuzzling between her legs as she bent down froze her heart. She screamed, dropping the bacon, and whirled round to see the alsatian skulking back to the two men standing behind with leering grins on their rough faces.

'I bet you thought your luck had changed,' one of them sniggered. The other man aimed a kick at the dog. 'You dirty bastard, you beat me to it.' They both giggled. She stood there, hands to her mouth, fists clenched.

'What the hell do you want?' she whispered, shocked and trembling.

'Oh… nothing darlin' nothing,' the younger one, Loon, said. She noticed his eyes and realised the skimpy little vest she was wearing didn't leave much hidden from the imagination. 'Who are you please?' she asked.

'We're your friendly neighbours,' Charlie Barsh said.

'Are you the men who spoke to my husband yesterday morning?'

She needed to mention Jack, to refer to him as her husband.

'Yes, me dear, you were snuggled up in the tent when we came visiting.' The big man smirked.

'We see you're rustlin' up some breakies. How 'bout being a little neighbourly and offering us some coffee?'

Loon moved closer, still looking at her breasts. She knew her nipples were standing out hard in the still cold air, and he was gazing straight through the thin material, almost slavering at the mouth.

'Okay,' she sighed, 'wait a minute.' She ducked inside the tent and pulled on a jumper over the vest, then stepped out again.

'Oh,' Charlie Barsh tutted. 'What a shame, that was a beautiful early morning view.'

Her blood raced with anger, but she was determined to remain cool, and spooned out some instant Nescafe into two cups, she handed them the coffees.

'Thank you darling, where is your man this morning?'

'He's gone for the newspapers.' She said, making herself busy with the utensils.

'Lucky boy to have such a lovely wife,' Loon said. 'thought he said you were his girlfriend?'

She whirled round, colour flaring at her cheeks. 'Look, you'll go too far in a minute, now drink up and please go.'

She stood up facing them, they grinned back.

'Only paying a compliment missus, very sorry.' Loon said, mockingly touching his forelock.

'We'll be off now,' they swallowed the coffee. 'Thanks again, and don't forget, if you need anything just look us up, we're just along the bank.'

'Yes, and if you ever get lonely, you know, if hubby's away…'

'Goodbye.' She cut in, and turned her back. She felt helpless, the tears were coming, and she couldn't control them. Sitting down on the grass, her head on her knees, she sobbed bitterly.

The bacon lay crisp and golden in the pan and the coffee was hot when she saw the car coming back and cracked the eggs into the pan.

He sensed something wrong immediately. 'What's up?'

She looked up at him and he could see her reddened eyes and nose. He dropped to his knees beside her. 'What's wrong?'

The tears started to well in her eyes again. 'Those men…'

'What men?' He shouted, his voice high pitched, feeling himself panic. He knew already who she was talking about.

'Those men you met yesterday.'

'Yes, yes, what happened?'

'Oh, nothing happened, they just scared me, and they were fucking rude.'

'What did they do?'

'Nothing… nothing… just the way they looked, the things they said, you know, crude remarks, all that shit. Anyway, what did Bell think about our sighting?' she said trying to change the subject.

'Fuck the sighting… what remarks, what did they say to you?' he demanded, his heart pounding with fear and rage. He grabbed her shoulders, shaking her.

'You're hurting me,' she shouted, 'look, it's not worth going over the nitty gritty, I just didn't like them, they scare me.'

'You wait here,' he grunted and walked off.

'Darling, please don't, we don't want any hassle,' she pleaded.

'No hassle, I'll be back in a minute.' He strode off.

The caravan was on the other side of a small copse about three hundred yards along the bank from their campsite. The rundown looking vehicle and its immediate surroundings was a shock to the eye, a raw sore in such stark contrast to its surrounding beauty. Litter was everywhere. Bottles, tin cans, newspapers, vegetable peelings, food cartons and rags were strewn all over the defaced ground, even tangled in the brambles and hanging from branches.

He could hear the screech of pop music from a transistor and the accompanying inane babble from an early morning DJ. He noticed the dog asleep on the ground between himself and the caravan. It was tethered by a long chain attached to a stake. He tried to work out the length of the chain, it didn't look long enough to allow the dog to reach the caravan door.

He decided to skirt round the edge of the area and approach the caravan from the other side, then nip round to the door without waking the dog. If it did wake, he hoped the chain would not be long enough.

As he reached the door, the dog woke and spotted him. It growled then dashed at him. He stood flattened against the caravan door, as the creature raced for him, then the chain snapped taut jerking the dog back just as it reached him. It stood there reared up on its hind legs, teeth bared, yapping and slavering barely a foot away from his face.

'You stupid cur!' He yelled, 'I'll kick your head in!' The door flew open, and he turned to see Charlie Barsh grinning down at him.

'Hello, my friend, come in,' the man yelled, and Jack stepped up into the caravan slamming the door shut on the dog's racket. The inside smells of the caravan hit him the moment he took his first breath in the gloomy interior. Stale tobacco, greasy cooking, and the odour of dirty bodies mingled together in a nauseating fug. He could also smell the dog, and guessed the creature must also sleep in there with them.

The transistor continued its crackling din as he took in the chaotic scene inside. Unmade bunks, dirty ashtrays and food plates everywhere, and clothes... hanging from everywhere, every available hook, dumped over chairs, bursting out of drawers and lying on the floor.

Loon, the younger brother, lounged on a bunk in a stained white tee shirt and jeans reading a comic.

'Well, if it ain't our jolly camper.' He grinned.

Jack's blood was already pumping, he'd promised himself to stay cool. He walked over and turned the transistor off.

'Now listen to me, you couple of scum. You've just scared the shit out of my woman!' He paused, waiting for a response. The one on the bed took a suck from a half pint bottle of Guinness, and the big man continued to lounge against the door, his thumbs tucked in his belt, the same grin on his face. Armstrong knew he had to get an impact across. 'That's the last time you come anywhere near our camp. You do so again, and I'll call the police.'

'You hear that Charlie?' Loon said, 'boy scout here is threatening us.' He said snorting into his beer.

'Well Loon, she is a pretty little thing, you can't really blame him for worrying about her.'

Loon's grin widened exposing nicotine stained teeth. 'No Charlie, we can't really blame him. Mister, if you don't like us as your neighbours, you'd best up and piss off. We've been here a long time and we're camped on private property that we got permission to sit on, so go get stuffed.' He spat the words out, still grinning.

Jack knew his threats had made an impact like a snowball in hell. 'You bastards… you've had your warning. Come mooching around my tent again and you'll be lucky if I call the fuzz… I'll take a 12 bore shotgun to you.'

He turned and walked to the door. Charlie slouched away and pulled the door open. Then Jack noticed the equipment hanging in the corner. Two wet suits, tubes, mouth pieces and regulators. His head spun, then his eyes caught the rest of the gear on the floor. Two sets of air tanks and valves. Masks, fins and spear guns.

The alsatian's yapping, as the door slammed behind him hardly penetrated his numbed senses as he walked round the end of the caravan.

He was making his way along the back of the vehicle when suddenly a back window burst open, jerking him out of his thoughts. As he spun round, he saw Loon's insane grinning face and the twin muzzles of a shotgun pointing at him, barely twelve inches from his face. He froze, cold fear gripping at his guts. Click, click… the two hammers fell on empty chambers.

Loon Barsh whooped with glee and bellowed hysterically. Armstrong could still hear their lunatic whooping as he made his way back through the trees to his tent.

The lounge bar of the Culloden Arms was empty at 12:30, still a little early for most of the coach parties and tourists to make their lunchtime stop. Jimmy Bell, however, was sitting in his usual place on the end bar stool when Jack and Tina walked in. They walked over to him.

'Same as last time?' he offered. 'Our shout.' Armstrong said

'How are you this morning?' He asked.

She sighed, 'Oh, pretty bloody fed up, to tell you the truth.'

'Oh… after Jack's awesome sighting?'

'But we've had a bad experience since then,' Jack said.

'Oh?' Bell sipped his drink.

'Do you know anything about a couple of brothers called Barsh?'

Bell swallowed quickly, 'Oh, oh, don't tell me you had a run in with the brothers Barsh already.'

'Yep,' Tina said.

'Jeez, you've certainly had a lively time since you arrived.'

'We're camped pretty well next door to them.' Jack said.

'Oh no, I didn't dream it was there, what's happened anyway?'

Jack swallowed a quarter of the pint, 'when I came to see you this morning,' Bell nodded, 'Teen was getting the breakfast when they dropped in and set about winding her up. You know, crude suggestions, all that crap. When I got back, she was sobbing her heart out.'

'Bastards.' Tina hissed under her breath.

'Anyway,' Jack said, 'I stormed over to their caravan and

threatened and shouted a bit, but I can't say that I made any kind of impression. They just grinned at me and took the piss.'

'Well, if it's any consolation,' Bell said, 'you're not the first to have that kind of run in with the Barsh's, they're a right pair of evil bastards. One of them is quite mad... should be locked up. I suggest you find another campsite.'

'But I don't want to. Why in hell's name should we move?'

Tina broke in. 'Jack, we're going to move, no way am I going to stay there.'

'Who are they Jimmy, can't they be told to get out of there by the police or the local council or something?' Jack asked. 'For God's sake their site is like a rubbish tip.'

'They can't be moved,' Bell said, 'there's a strip of beach that runs from the road down to the water which belongs to old man Dunbar. You may have heard of him. His home is on the other side of Foyers Road. The land is like an extension of his gardens and he owns it. They live there rent free.'

'Shit, why the hell does he allow them to squat there?'

'I think I'd better fill you in on the whole scene.'

'Yeah, sounds like a damn good idea.' Tina said.

'Have you heard the legend of the lost Culloden treasure?'

'You mean, Charlie's Gold?' she broke in.

'That's right,' Bell smiled, 'who told you about?'

'Red Angus,' Jack replied, 'according to him the favourite theory is that it's somewhere at the bottom of the loch.'

'And right here, some say,' Bell said, 'somewhere in or around this establishment. There are many old stories which seem to suggest that two wounded clansmen stopped off here and had their wounds tended. They had with them the famous treasure. It was during their stay here that the innkeeper hid the gold for them on the promise of a third of the share-out later. The two clansmen were killed shortly afterwards, and the landlord was killed a few days later when the real butchery started in the months following the battle... or so the story goes. That's just one of the stories.'

'So that gold could be anywhere,' Jack murmured, 'in the loch, under our feet somewhere, or maybe it was shared out by a hundred drunken Redcoats back in the 18th century.'

'Yep, that's about the gist of it, but I must add, the greatest weight of opinion is that it is in the loch, and that's the opinion of some very informed people, people who have devoted years of their lives to it. Old Dunbar, for example.'

'Right, that's where we came in.'

'Well, Dunbar is really into Charlie's Gold, in fact I would say he is the most ruthlessly avid treasure hunter of them all. He really has made a complete study of the legend. He's been searching now for the past twenty years. He's getting on for seventy years now, but until recently he was diving himself. Now he hires the likes of the Barsh brothers.'

'So that's it,' Jack said, 'I saw their equipment this morning, now it makes sense.'

'Now you know, and now you know why it would be impossible to kick them out.'

'Well that's no problem,' Tina said, 'we'll just get out. I don't mind somewhere else, this side of the loch maybe, but at least a few miles between them and us.'

Jack sighed. 'But what's the point of that, the whole idea is to stick around the spot where we've had the two best sightings ever. There must be a reason why it keeps popping up there, and I want to know why.'

'Coincidence!' She burst out, 'bloody coincidence, that's all!' She was on the point of tears.

'Okay baby,' he put his arm round her, 'no use rucking, nothing's worth that.'

Tina sat bolt upright on her stool, her hands clenched on her knees, her temple pounding with rage.

'Maybe after what you said Jack,' Bell said, trying to ease the tension, 'with you going around to their caravan and all, perhaps they'll stay away for a while.'

Jack finished his pint and stood up. 'Come on darling,' he took her hand, she stood up and finished her drink.

'See you both soon and look after yourselves.'

'Bye,' she smiled.

She started crying as soon as they shut themselves into the car.

'Hey cool it,' he moved across and put his hand on the nape of her neck under her hair. 'I don't want anything to come between us.'

'Oh, what's the point in saying things like that. You want to do it, and you're going to do it, I'm just terrified.'

'I can't force you to stay there.'

'And I can't force you to leave,' she wiped her eyes, 'we'll stay for a while and see what happens.'

'We'll give it a week. I'll start diving tomorrow, and if I can't find anything in a week, we'll leave.'

She blew her nose. 'And if anything bad happens, we'll go right away, okay?'

'It's a deal,' he said solemnly.

She looked at him and managed a tear-stained smile.

Half an hour later they were pulling up at the bottom of a dirt track at the water's edge near the southern end of the loch. A couple of land-rovers, a big caravan, an assortment of other vehicles and four boats huddled at the end of a wooden jetty.

'They're diving over there.' Jack pointed out over the water.

Tina could see a big yellow plastic or fibre glass raft with a couple of men in wetsuits sitting on it amongst piles of equipment.

'The divers are down at the moment, you can just see their bubbles… one, two, three,' he counted the separate clusters of air breaking the surface. 'There are three men working below.'

Other people were busy around the outfit. They could hear the purr of a compressor as two men filled tanks. Other people were standing round in groups, there were children playing and even a woman hanging out washing outside one of the caravans. They wondered if all those people were part of the diving team, or whether some of them were tourists just hanging round to watch. They walked onto the jetty and the two men at the compressor looked up.

'Hi,' Jack greeted.

'Hello,' one of them, a tanned lean man in his mid-thirties stood up smiling. 'Can I help you?' he asked in an American drawl.

'Well, I hope you can,' Jack held out his hand, 'my name's Jack Armstrong, this is my girlfriend Tina.' They shook hands. 'I'm diving on the other side of the loch, at least intending to start diving, and I'm looking for air.'

'You've got no compressor, or your compressor broke down?'

'Got no compressor at the moment,' Jack said, 'but I'm getting one as soon as I can.'

'You're welcome to our air buddy, for as long as you like. We'll have to charge you a nominal something to cover costs,' the man said.

'That's great,' Jack grinned.

'What about that old machine?' another man broke in.

'Yeah, that's an idea, we've got an old Seibe-Gorman we don't use anymore. There's nothing wrong with it, maybe we can sell it to you.'

'Yeah, great, where is it?' Jack asked.

The compressor was in the back of one of the land-rovers and seemed in good enough condition although looking well used. Jack knew he would sort out any problems with it if there were any, he'd worked with Seibe-Gorman equipment for all his diving life.

'What do you want for it?'

'Oh, I dunno… twenty?'

'Done.' Jack said.

'Don't you wanna try it out?' the man asked.

'No, don't worry, I'll soon iron out any kinks, if there are any.'

'You a pro-diver?' the man asked.

'I was… offshore oil, just finished with the North Sea.'

'Oh, so you should know how to get the old Seibe-Gorman started,' the man joked. 'Excuse me for prying, but I guess I'm naturally nosey. What are you going for, monster or treasure?'

'Monster.'

'What got you interested? People don't go to the lengths I suspect you're going to unless something really happens.'

'We've had a couple of very good sightings.' Jack said.

'That's a good excuse for a drink, come on and tell us all about it, we're always interested in new sightings.' He led them into one of the caravans.

'What'll you have?' he rummaged on a shelf piled with books, papers, maps and boxes of Kodak film. The interior was crammed with equipment for the expedition. Rubber suits, air tanks and hoses were piled up and hanging everywhere amidst fishing rods, nets, coils of rope, pulleys and hooks. Cardboard boxes and tea chests were stacked ceiling high, their labels suggesting photographic equipment, diving spares and canned foods.

He picked up three glasses, clunking them together with three fingers, and three cans of Shlitz. 'There we go,' he said with a grin, 'cheers.'

'Cheers.' They both replied.

They told him everything about their experience. He was astounded, particularly with that morning's story.

'Shit, excuse me Ma'am, but what you saw this morning, has got to be positively historic, the monster actually picking the goose outta the air like that! He let out a load whistle. 'Have you told anybody yet?'

'Only Jimmy Bell up at the Bureau.'

'Oh yes, Jim's an old college buddy of mine from back home. Nice guy, totally dedicated to Nessie.'

'Can't see the point in telling anybody else, we've got no proof or eyewitnesses.'

'Yeah, that's the damn pity, your two sightings have got to be the best ever, if only you'd managed a decent shot.'

'When you look at the time, the man hours, and the money spent on this outfit, and then look at the actual physical proof.' He shook his head.

'Is it true what they say about the visibility, is it always bad because of the peat content?' Jack asked.

'Yeah, that's the whole damn problem,' he said, 'it's as black as night down there. You descend below fifteen feet and you're descending into a black void. I'm warning you now, it's scary.'

'Well, what have you seen?' Tina asked.

'We haven't seen anything, not underwater anyway. All of us have had surface sightings.'

'Anything good?'

'No, nothing exceptional, certainly nothing comparable to what you describe. Just the usual upturned boat shape on numerous occasions, a couple of distant head and necks, and various humps. Always the usual problem though, distance, either that or the suddenness of the appearance, and the just as quick disappearance.'

'Don't we know.'

'I know we all would have seen plenty underwater if the visibility was good. You see, we've had very close contact with the creature.'

Tina shuddered, 'What do you mean?'

'It's difficult to explain until you experience it yourself. Down there in the black it's just... I don't know, a feeling maybe a swirl, a surge of water pressure, something so powerful it can bowl you over. One or two of us have been touched, we know it's not ordinary fish or sunken logs. The sheer weight and living power is such that it can't be anything else. I've felt it, but it's hard to explain. Maybe you'll know yourself soon.'

'God, now you've got me really wetted, I can't wait to get under there.' Jack grinned. Tina sighed and looked away.

'You'll change your mind the first time it happens to you I promise you. My first time, I kicked upward so fast they mistook me for Polaris.'

'How come you're still diving if you've realised there's no way you're going to see the creature underwater?' Jack asked, 'especially as you've had physical contact and still seen nothing. I don't see the point.'

'Bones,' he said. 'we've given up the idea of any underwater sightings, the whole campaign has switched to the search for skeletal remains. Up till now the greatest mystery of the Loch Ness phenomenon is that burning question. What happens to the remains of the creatures when they die? The sceptic will always argue that there should have been some skeletal remains found if we are to believe that an unknown species has inhabited the loch since pre-history. Not even an unexplained toenail has ever been found.'

'So those guys out there are searching the bottom for bones?' Jack said.

'Yep, underwater archaeology, we're scanning the bottom inch by inch. Raking, sifting and digging. You never know, we might come across Charlie's Gold while we're about it,' he laughed. 'monster or treasure, either one can make a man damned rich.'

'Who is financing all this if it's not a rude question?' Jack ventured.

'It's backed privately by a millionaire back in Fort Worth, Texas. He has been obsessed with the Loch Ness monster since he came here on a holiday back in the fifties. He and his wife had a pretty good sighting, and he's had the bug ever since. Ever since then he has always vowed to do all he can to solve the mystery... come up with concrete proof. He has ploughed all his spare cash into this outfit. Yep, the old man has spent thousands of dollars, maybe millions on this project, and he ain't about to give up now.'

'How come,' Jack said, 'we've been here a couple of days and we manage to get two of the best sightings out of the lot of you?'

'It's either luck, or there is something living near your camp-site, anyway, don't forget, it's physical proof this outfit's after, that's where the dollars are going.'

'It's still depressing to think that someone's been searching and spending money like that for nigh on thirty bloody years and still has nothing to show for it.'

'One question,' the man asked, 'your campsite area, where is it?'

'Hmm, I reckon, standing at Urquhart Castle, it would be eleven o'clock on the opposite bank.'

'That's near old Dunbar's place. You come across the Barshes?'

'Yes.' They both said in unison.

'Well keep clear of them, they're not nice.'

'Thanks,' she said, 'we gathered that.'

'Anyway, your campsite… you looked at the maps in the Bureau no doubt, is it a favourite sighting spot?'

'No, it's not, but Bell's theory is that the reason is because the banks are so steep and wooded there. The water is impossible to see from the bank.'

'Okay,' the man said, looking at his watch, 'I gotta go, but listen, take my advice and be careful, you know the rules, you shouldn't be diving on your own.'

CHAPTER FIVE

The steady sound of his breathing through the aqualung valve seemed to echo loud and hollow in the darkness all around him. He looked up and saw his bubbles, yellow in the peaty water, wobbling big and fat towards the surface. He was twenty feet down, and visibility was almost gone. All he could see in front of him were the eerie shapes of the ridges, holes and overhangs of the loch side, and below, the beckoning blackness of the deep. He thought of the North Sea and the great depths he had dived there, remembering that at this depth there would be noise, turbulence and so much light in the clear water. Never had he experienced the utter gloomy stillness he was now passing through. A deep sense of foreboding, of lurking danger enveloped him. The smell of the loch seeped through his facemask. Millions of years of stillness, of ancient peat, of rotted vegetation mingled with the stench and taste of fear forced him to fight the almost uncontrollable urge to kick for the surface.

He wondered how far above the bottom he was. Looking down he saw the tops of long black weeds rising out of the blackness and guessed the bottom couldn't be far. Perhaps another thirty feet. He hovered, wanting to persuade himself he'd have another go tomorrow. He thought of Tina sitting in the warm sunlight, gazing at his bubbles, worrying. Cursing himself, telling himself he was one of the top pros in the world, he jack-knifed and slid down into the jungle of slime and weeds.

Reaching the bottom, feet first, he found himself up to his waist in mud which billowed up around him, filling his nostrils with the stench of decay. Above him was a haze of brownish, yellow light and around him he could see nothing, just feel the jungle of matted vegetation, the slime and the intense cold. He decided to explore the immediate surroundings, say roughly about four hundred square feet, then call it a day. He felt himself losing his battle with fear. Kicking free of the ooze and about six feet off the bottom to avoid disturbing the mud, he began very gently swimming through the weeds and screens of hanging slime. So far he hadn't bothered to use his torch. Experience told him that with water so congested, the light would just bounce back at him like a car's headlights in a fog. He decided to give it a try anyway. He depressed the rubber switch with his thumb and the light exploded all around him, reflecting off the millions of peat particles. A myriad of tiny fish scattered like a fireworks cascade, their silver sides flashing before disappearing into the darkness. He thought he saw the flashing flanks of another larger fish to his right but couldn't be sure. A salmon or perhaps a char he thought. Slowly he moved through the darkness, the weeds slipping over his body, clinging to him then reluctantly losing their grip. Occasionally he'd find himself pushing through congested masses of substance. Decaying vegetation, dead weeds, rotted surface algae, all hanging motionless in the thick water just above the bottom.

For a full five minutes he quartered a rough area of four hundred square feet, then decided enough was enough. He decided to go back to the loch wall and inspect that on the way up. He knew Tina would be worried, but she would be ok so long as she could see his bubbles.

He estimated to be about thirty yards from the shore and shone the torch before turning back. He suddenly noticed a void immediately ahead. Although the visibility was hopeless, he had been able to see weeds in the immediate few feet around him, but here suddenly was this nothingness. He kicked gently forward into the emptiness, and immediately sensed the absence of the bottom, he was in a void. Suspended and hovering, he shone the torch downwards, nothing. He then moved backwards and touched bottom and weed again. He realised he was on the edge of a precipice, a ledge that gave way to the real yawning depths. He moved gradually down off the ledge, and down the precipice wall for a few yards. He thought of the hundreds of feet of dark water below him and he froze, fighting the panic. The urge to move upwards towards that yellow haze, towards warmer water, to sunlight was too much to fight. Back to the surface of this terrifying loch, back to its surface of holidaymakers, pleasure boats, the laughter of kids. He pushed backwards away from the wall of the chasm and kicked gently towards the light.

He spat out his mouthpiece and lifted his mask the instant he broke surface. The water felt like a warm bath as he lay back into the luxury of it, his face to the sun.

'You ok?'

'Yeah,' he shouted back through numbed lips. Still floating on his back, he kicked slowly towards her.

'Help me out… I'm shagged.'

He crawled through the shallows on hands and knees.

'Jees, you stink,' she said, 'how was it?'

He lay on the pebbles feeling sick with cold and exhaustion. 'Get me a cuppa first,' he gasped.

'The kettle's been singing ever since you went down,' she said. 'Plenty of sugar please baby.'

To him there was never anything as good as a big mug of hot sweet tea after a heavy dive. He knew from experience that alcohol of any kind was wrong. It thinned the blood, and the old idea of having a tot of something when desperately cold was a foolish and dangerous one.

'I'll wash down... get all this muck off. Shit, I do smell a bit.'

'A bit? Wow!' She laughed.

He stood under the cascading burn that tumbled down the hillside while it cleansed him of the horrors of the Loch Ness bottom.

He told her about the dive while they ate lunch, a couple of packets of Vesta curry and rice, made hotter with a liberal sprinkling of cayenne pepper.

'So what you're trying to say is that you'd like to explore the wall of that chasm?' She felt herself sound like she was beginning to nag. All the feelings of apprehension came back stronger now he'd described the dive. She wanted more than ever to plead with him again to abandon the whole thing, but she fought to stay calm.

'Look baby, is there really much point in diving, you can't see anything for God's sake.' She wondered if that sounded like a nag.

'Yeah, I think there is a point, don't start getting fidgety again.' He smiled and pinched her cheek.

She moved into his arms, her face buried in his shoulder.

'When I was down there,' he said, 'you wouldn't believe how much I longed to be up here... just like this... nice and close, and warm.'

'When are you going down again?'

'Right now,' he grunted, squeezing her against him, 'right now. We'll zip up the tent, there's nobody about...'

'Shut up, you over-sexed sod.'

'What are we going to do for the rest of the day?' she asked.

'Well, I've had enough today, it's gonna take me a day to get my guts back to go down there again, so how's about getting in the car and going for a drive? Have a drink somewhere.'

'Tell you what we could do,' she said, ' how about visiting the Culloden battlefield.'

'Yeah, great idea, it's only a few miles. But let's find a nice quiet pub somewhere first, I could do with a few pints.'

Culloden Moor, the scene of the last great battle on British soil in 1746, lies about five miles to the south-east of the highland capital of Inverness. After a drink they took a leisurely drive to the battlefield and found it at the roadside, a stone memorial cairn marking the spot where the battle was supposed to have been thickest. Stone walls criss-crossed the landscape, rising, falling and disappearing at times with the swell of the moor, and patches of forestry pine in neat blocks spoiling and subduing the old wild moor, cutting and trimming it to size, husbanding the old wilderness and its bloody past.

They parked the VW and got out breathing in the thick buttery smell of gorse which was abundant over the battlefield. They walked towards the memorial cairn. A large plaque set in the rocks told them,

'*The Battle of Culloden was fought on this moor*
16th April 1746. The graves of the gallant

*highlanders who fought for Scotland and Prince Charlie
are marked by the names of their clans.'*

'All this must have looked a lot different at the time of the battle,' Jack said. 'In 1746, it would have been a bleak and treeless moorland, broken only with freezing bogs and rough stone or turf dykes.'

They walked to the little white stone cottage standing in isolation away from the road and carpark.

'This is Old Leanach,' he said as they stepped in.

'How come you're such an expert?' she asked.

'I'm not really, it's just that I once happened to read a very good book on all this by John Prebble. Since then I've been fascinated.'

The interior was a cool white painted main room with displays in glass cabinets, and relics from the battle hung around the walls. A warden sat by the door.

'It's fascinating to think that this cottage was in the middle of all the fighting,' she whispered.

'Yeah, this is where it all happened. There was an old barn at the back of this place where one of the most barbaric acts of atrocity took place. Apparently about thirty highlanders took refuge in the barn. Instead of the English soldiers just shooting them when they found them, they barricaded up the barn doors and set fire to it, roasting the poor devils alive.'

'Nice.'

'Hey, look at this,' she pulled him to a glass cabinet next to the big old fireplace. A small hand painted sign on the glass read: 'THE LOST TREASURE OF BONNIE PRINCE CHARLIE'. They both bent over the exhibit intently. Most of the material included typewritten sheets, a few sections of maps, a couple of engravings and a miniature or two of the Prince. Nothing new except for one item that eventually drew their interest.

It was an old book, very thick and displayed open on a spread dealing with the lost treasure.

They both lowered their faces nearer the glass, reading with great difficulty the very small type. The book had been published in the 19th Century, and the story was told in typical Victorian style.

Most of the pages were filled with long references to dates and places, and large paragraphs dealing with land rights and descriptions of events, mainly legal, in connection with the long and confused aftermath of the battle. It was only towards the end of the two pages that reference began to be made concerning the English Government searches for the legendary gold, then end of the page...

'I don't believe it,' she laughed.

Jack glanced across at the warden sitting by the door. 'Excuse me, I wonder if you could help us.' He walked over to the man and smiled.

'We are both students from London. We're studying the history of the Jacobite Rebellion. It's just that we were studying your exhibit concerning the lost treasure of Bonnie Prince Charlie and we are most interested in the next page.'

'You want it turned over?' the man smiled. Within five minutes they were bending over the book again reading the next page.

'Nice man.' Tina giggled. 'Shut up and read on.' Jack whispered.

...was said to have been revealed to the mistress of a clansman who had gone to his doom with the Prince's gold strapped to his

person in a money belt, the person who had made this revelation having been with the doomed clansman and had witnessed the latter's heinous murder.

The aforesaid mistress being frequently influenced by home-made mountain whisky prompt mislaid the exact information intrusted to her. She died some few months later, be it also at the hands of the rampaging English redcoats, many hundreds of which still roamed the highlands intoxicated with rape, plunder and blood lust yet not sated.

However, the comely wench once spoke to the grandfather of a friend of the author of this publication who by chance dwelled not more than a mile from the great loch. The story she related is as the following:

Her lover, the dead clansman was attempting to row a boat from Ruthven Jetty in flight from a gang of murdering English redcoats. The said clansman had on his person the gold of Bonnie Prince Charlie securely strapped to his middle in an ample money belt. Together with him were two worthy comrades, one of which being the eye witness who had related the tale to the drunken wench after bringing her the sad tidings of her lover's demise.

When the rowing boat had progressed to some one hundred yards or more from the jetty, the murderous band opened musket fire at the trio in the boat. With leaden ball all around them, they continued to row in the hope of moving out of range of the musketry.

Just when they had started to row out of musket range and the lead balls began to fall short of their quarry, the man with the money belt entertained a mortal head wound which toppled the latter overboard and into the depths. Soon another clansman was killed, leaving the one to escape to tell his tale.

His tale continues to tell that the trio had made a direct course

*to the jetty at Castle Urquhart, where some score of survivors from
the battle had congregated in refuge.*

*The above had been duly recorded in writing by one or other of
the original listeners of this historic tale.*

'Excuse me again,' he asked the man at the door. 'that book…
how long has it been part of the exhibition?'

'Two days.'

'Do you know where it came from?'

'No, I don't concern myself.'

They began to realise that the old boy had clearly done his
helpful deed for the day.

'It's important to us.' Armstrong urged.

'I don't know I'm telling yer. The wee man comes down now
and again and puts things into the glass case and takes things
away… I don't know.'

'What wee man?'

'Och… he comes from Fort George.'

On the drive back to the loch, their talk was not about the
mysterious creature that they knew lived in its black waters,
but the suddenly more fascinating and mysterious Charlie's
Gold that they were now sure lay hiding itself among the eels
and the mud of the loch bottom.

'It did seem incredibly convincing didn't it?' Tina said, breaking the silence of their thoughts.

'Yes, it did. To think the story actually came from the mouth
of an eyewitness. Somebody who was actually there and saw
the money belt itself go overboard.'

'How come nobody else has stumbled across this information? It seems that with everything we do around here,

we're doing better than anybody else. After only being here a couple of days, we see the monster twice, and better than anybody else... then this. Sounds too good to be true... all of it,' she said.

'Come on baby, have a bit of faith in lady luck. I reckon we've just been lucky. Coincidence if you like, you said that yourself yesterday. Besides the story about the clansmen in the rowing boat sinking with the gold is one of the more common theories, after all, Red Angus told us about that one the first day we met him. It's the bit about the location, this Ruthven Jetty.'

'It's still a bit of a long shot,' Tina sighed, 'what with drunken wenches, and friends of friends of grandfathers etc etc, whoever did write that stuff?'

'Yeah, yeah, I know, it's still bloody exciting babe.'

'Do you think the money belt would have rotted away by now?' Tina asked, gazing out of the open window at the hills and mountains on the blue horizon that seemed to move ponderously in the opposite direction to the rushing trees and rocks in the immediate foreground.

'Not necessarily. The chemical content of the water plays a great part in the length of life of something like that which has been submerged for so long. My guess is that it's down there somewhere, completely intact, but the minute it is touched it would disintegrate.'

He winked at her, squeezing her thigh and at the same time changing gear to take the steep climb up the side of the valley. Giant grey boulders hung over the road from the mountainside above, and to the left the ground gave way to the desolation of scree and then the purple moorland of Drummossie.

He looked down and across the rugged landscape, his

imagination speeding back the two centuries to the bloody times of Culloden. He could see the straggling groups of defeated highlanders. Wild, starving, many grievously wounded and sick. Struggling through the freezing bogs to escape the bayonets of the drunken and vengeful English Redcoats bearing down on them from horseback. The butchers of the power mad Duke of Cumberland, and the government who spent the hundred years after the battle clearing the highlands of the proud men of the clans, abandoned by their own Bonnie Prince.

He sighed. 'To think it was practically genocide. The English were definitely the villains. The clans had been a nuisance and a threat, and they had to be eliminated.'

She gazed out across the wild scene.

'Do you know,' he said, breaking into her thoughts. 'Cumberland went back to London after the battle to a hero's welcome. Cheering crowds lining the streets, the lot. As far as the English public knew, he had saved the country from an invasion. He was feted and applauded wherever he went and was bestowed the Governorship of Inverness Castle and the title of Baron Culloden. There was a service of thanksgiving at St. Paul's and Handel was commissioned to compose 'See the conquering hero comes.'

'You really have read up on all this,' she said.

'You know the flower, Sweet William?' he said, 'the grateful English public named it after him. And here in Scotland they named the same flower after him. They called it 'Stinking Billy'.

Okay, back to business. How do we propose acting on all this new information we've just come across?' he said.

'I think, number one is we'd better make up our minds what the hell we're looking for, monsters or gold. We've got to decide and concentrate on one thing.'

'Yeah,' he sighed, 'I suppose my interest in the monster has waned a bit after that dive. I don't mind admitting I was terrified down there,' he shuddered at the memory of the cold terror of the loch depths.

'Don't worry,' she sighed, 'I'm just as scared for you as you are for yourself.'

'I must say, what we turned up this afternoon is more than a bit interesting. It's all eyewitness stuff.'

'Well, it seems incredible, but it certainly looks like we are the first people to have read that passage in the book for a very long time.'

'If we could just pinpoint the spot at which our man went down with the money belt.'

'If, if, if,' she moaned

CHAPTER SIX

He had been lying on his back under the tent canvas, listening to the deep steady breathing of her sleep and watching the grey white glow of the moon through the canvas. She had been asleep for almost two hours, and now at last the crowding thoughts of his insomnia had begun to take shape. Cloudy images from two hundred years ago... the gang of Redcoats on Ruthven Jetty... the fleeing clansmen in a small rowing boat amidst whistling lead ball and shot... the boat pulling out of range... a Redcoat squinting along the long barrel of his musket for a last shot... a puff of smoke... a toppling figure, a rocking boat and a splash. Suddenly it was there in clear, sharp focus. The idea.

The early morning sun appeared like the blaze of a forest fire through the timber high up on the hills across the loch, its colours reflecting rose pink and crimson on the wispy flecks of cirrus cloud. Thin rays of sunlight reached across and splashed the waking loch and its glen, filling Red Angus's cove and campsite with light and warmth. The big man yawned, shaking his great head, the copper curls catching fire in the slanting rays of the sunrise.

'Out with it then, tell me all about this great idea.' He grumbled, stirring heaped teaspoons of Nescafe Gold Blend into steaming mugs.

They told him everything about the visit to the battlefield, their discovery in Old Leanach, and the account of the shooting and the man and money belt going to the bottom of the loch on the way across from Ruthven Jetty.

'Well, it's a new one on me,' he grunted, 'everyone's heard about the story of the clansman and the gold going down to the bottom, but there's never any info on the exact location.'

'That's just it,' Jack said. 'The old book has only just been exhibited and was put on display a couple of days ago. It looks like we may be the only people aware of it.'

'Come on then… what's your idea?' the Scotsman grumbled impatiently.

'Okay, here it is,' Jack went straight into his theory, 'let's say we accept the story, the eyewitness account telling us that a man with a money belt full of gold coin was shot at with musket fire while rowing away from Ruthven Jetty on a straight course for Urquhart Castle across the loch. Then, as they were pulling out of musket range he was hit and toppled into the water, the heavy money belt taking him straight to the bottom of the loch.' He looked at Red Angus searching for a hint of encouragement in the rugged face.

'Well, don't you see? It's bloody simple… when they were pulling out of musket range, that's the important bit. We just get hold of the right kind of musket, stand on the end of Ruthven Jetty, fire a few balls in a straight line to towards Urquhart Castle, and mark the spot where the balls drop. That would be the spot, give or take a few yards, when the boat would have been moving out of range… the moment when the guy with the money belt went overboard. We then start diving in a twenty yard radius from that spot… simple!'

Red Angus sat on a boulder, his head resting on his hands

in silence for a full ten seconds.

Jack waited for the response.

'Umm, not bad,' he looked up, 'but only one snag.'

'What?'

'What if your spot is over 800 feet of water?'

'We'll solve that problem if and when it happens.' Jack smiled triumphantly. 'In the meantime, are you with us Red? We'll need you, besides, can you get hold of the right musket?'

Red stood up, then his face creased into a great grin.

'Of course you're gonna need me, you two ain't capable of looking after yourselves.'

Jack laughed and thrust his hand into the vice-grip.

'I have an old army chum at Fort George, he looks after the museum there. It has an excellent collection of Culloden relics. Yes, I can get the musket.'

Later that morning Red Angus got astride the big old Harley Davidson and roared off to Fort George on the west coast. Tina and Jack went back to the campsite. 'How about getting a picnic lunch together and spending a lazy day?' Jack suggested.

'Let's go to Ruthven Jetty,' she said.

'Great! Let's take the fishing rods.'

The jetty was about a mile and a half south along the bank and they took the car. They'd wanted to walk along the shore but realised they may encounter the Barshes.

They found the jetty in a rocky cove, a crumbling stone promontory reaching out like a broken finger into the tranquil water of a natural harbour, sheltered by a hillside of alder, larch and pine.

'It's beautiful… so peaceful.'

'There's Urquhart Castle,' he pointed across the water diagonally. The mirror image of its ruined turrets reflected in perfect symmetry in the slate smooth surface. 'It's a good coupla miles from here.'

'Urquhart Castle… Castle Urquhart, which is it?' Tina questioned.

'Dunno, whatever.'

They spent the afternoon happily snatching tiddler roach and rudd by dangling light line and tiny hooks off the jetty while lying on their stomachs and gazing down into the green water at the swarms of tiny fish feeding from the moss on the ancient stonework.

The afternoon dragged drowsily into evening, and before they realised it, the sun had slipped quietly behind the mountains on the other side of the loch.

'Time we made a move.' Jack said.

'Yeah, it's been a cracking day, peaceful, wonder if Red's got back yet.' Although she had been at peace that afternoon, and happy with Jack, there were times when her thoughts had wondered back to Red Angus.

As they made their way up the track to the road, they could almost feel the loch saying goodnight. They stopped and looked back. The dozing of a motor launch engine being eased into her overnight berth in some mist shrouded pier far across the loch drifted up to them, and the plaintive cry of an eagle somewhere up in the crags.

Then the phut, phut of a boat engine wafted across the water surface.

'It's Red,' she cried excitedly and pointed, a vague feeling of pleasure tightening inside her.

Jack's gaze caught the little yellow boat as it cut into the reflection of Urquhart Castle, its wake destroying the perfect image for a few moments.

The figure in the boat waved, then the guttural voice floated across obviously long seconds after it had left the mouth of Red Angus. The boat was still a half mile away, the mountains behind them catching the sound and bouncing it around a few times.

'Helloo-oo, helloo-o-lo…' They waved back. Soon they were helping to pull the boat up onto the shingle.

'Sorry to have been such a long time me bairns, but this beauty was a little more difficult to get hold of than I imagined. This is the famous Brown Bess.' He pulled the long firearm from under some oilskins at the bottom of the boat.

'Wow,' Jack exclaimed, as Red thrust the musket at him, 'it's heavy,' he said as he raised it to his shoulders, bet its difficult to keep steady on a target.'

'Especially in a freezing blizzard and up to your knees in a bog with grape shot singing around your head,' chuckled the Scotsman.

'Sometimes, of course, they supported these guns on metal rods they stuck into the ground, if they had the time that is. Bit different when there's a hoard of screaming clansmen charging down on you.'

'Have you got the ammunition or whatever you need for the thing?' Tina asked.

'Yeah darlin' got it all here.' Red Angus said, patting a big leather bag.

'Well then, there's nothing to stop us starting right away.' Armstrong said.

'Och, yes there is.' Red growled. 'I haven't eaten all day. I set off for Inverness at first light to pick up this gun, and I've only had a cup of coffee. Let's go back to your place first, I'm absolutely starving.'

'Okay,' Tina said, 'I'll rustle something up... there's only tinned stuff though.'

'Don't worry.' Red chuckled, pulling three wood pigeon from a canvas holdall. I'm cooking.'

Jack smiled. 'When did you get those?'

'Well,' Red's eyes twinkled mischievously. She thought how much she'd grown to love that twinkle that so changed his rough face.

'On the way back, with this beast slung across my back I just couldn't resist having myself a blast.' They both laughed. 'You mean, you killed those pigeons with that?'

'Yep, one can load these old guns in different ways you know, I just rammed in loose birdshot. I've got a secret little 'woodie' haunt I visit regularly,' he laughed.

Ok, I'll drive the beetle, back. You carry on with Red in the boat.' Teen.

'She's safe with me... Haha!' Red growled with a grin.

Soon they were chugging along the bank towards the campsite. 'We'll be passing the campsite of those bastards in a minute,' she said, 'it's just round that outcrop.'

'They're nothing to worry about. You just let me know if they cause you any bother and they'll answer to me,' he growled, 'I'm just waiting to find an excuse to use their livers as bait.'

'You had a run in with them?' she asked.

'No, but I've heard stories. They're looking for the gold and nothing or nobody's going to come in their way. They'll start snooping around once we start diving, but just let them go any further.'

Rounding the bend, they found themselves gliding across a small bay protected by huge granite overhangs. 'Och, God, what a mess,' Red grunted as the tawdry campsite of the Barsh's appeared in a cluster of young spruce. From the water, the whole seedy vision could be seen in all its glory. There was the main caravan, it seemed to be listing over to one side with a pile of logs taking the place of one of its wheels. Clothes and litter were strewn and hanging everywhere, just as it was when Armstrong last visited them. A horse was there, hobbled, head bowed and waiting for its next session of maltreatment in dumb resignation. The german shepherd had seen them and was throttling itself to get at them. As the boat moved further across the bay and clear of the trees, their eyes were greeted with a special sight. There squatting on his haunches was Charlie Barsh, his trousers round his ankles, relieving his bowels. He'd had his back to them but turned as he heard the motor. Then deliberately standing to face them full frontal, he grabbed his genitals gesturing obscenely as he arched backward, knees bent, screaming in shrill laughter.

Red Angus just bellowed with laughter, arching backwards himself with glee.

Tina stared, mouth open, incredulous, her gaze taking in the scene.

'That ain't much to be proud of!' Red shouted. 'I'll be showing you something in a moment that'll soon put that little thing to shame.' As he lifted his kilt and gestured, his coarse laughter booming against the overhanging cliffs.

'Oh God, look what…' she was pointing at the bank.

The other brother had come out from the caravan. He was staggering, a bottle in his hand. Charlie was still standing there, hands on hips now, still displaying his all. Brother Loon was bending over searching the debris around him frantically. Suddenly he picked up a flat piece of timber and staggered over to the spot where Charlie had been defecating.

'You hang on a second, I have a present for you. This'll make you smell nice lady!' he bayed with moronic laughter.

Red was enjoying every second.

Bending over and fumbling drunkenly, Loon had managed to scoop the muck onto one end of the plank. With this, the other Barsh convulsed into hysterics again.

'Aim well Loony me boy, don't waste it, I can't do no more, straight off.'

Then Loon Barsh, in the best college girl lacrosse style, heaved the shit in a lob towards them. It fell short, breaking up and splattering over the water between them. 'You're lucky that didn't hit us boys,' Red shouted, 'lucky indeed.'

'For God's sake, let's get out of here Red,' Tina screamed. She was crying now. 'You're enjoying every bloody minute of this, aren't you?' she sobbed.

'Sssh… no point getting upset over those scum.' Red growled.

She wondered in her sobs what was really upsetting her. After all, she'd seen and experienced and was used to all the indignities that men were capable of. She knew she was more upset with Red Angus, his display of coarseness, his obvious glee at the situation. She longed for his other side, the gentleness, that she knew was hidden inside him somewhere, she wanted to be in his arms right at that moment. She let herself go, her sobs racking her body.

'Yes, my love,' Red shouted, 'I loved every minute, but I tell you, if that shit had hit us... then the fun would have really started.' He put the outboard into a higher rev and the little boat lifted its bow and was soon purring past the next outcrop of bank and out of that sordid bay.

'I'm not really sure I can eat anything.' She said weakly as Red Angus deftly finished plucking and gutting the three wood pigeons and was singeing off the remaining stubble from the plump little bodies over the fiercely burning fire.

'You just wait a little while, old Red Angus is cooking now.' Armstrong was back with the car and they sat and watched him, two large whiskies in their hands. He'd bought a bottle of Glenfiddich. 'You just knock those wee drams back, it'll calm you down.'

He had skewered all three birds onto a stick and was placing them onto two forked sticks over the fire. Her mind was still on the disgusting incident of only half an hour ago, her stomach still in a tight knot, and a faint feeling of nausea in the solar plexus. She knew she couldn't face the wood pigeon.

Red made some final adjustments to the barbecue, then backed away from it proudly and sat down with them.

'There now, where's me drink?'

Within minutes the birds were beginning to brown, their carcasses glistening, the greases oozing and beginning to sputter over the intense heat. The scotch had already started to envelope them in its comforting glow. They were already beginning to relax again. Half an hour and a couple of large whiskies later, the three pigeons were done. Firm and brown on their skewer, their delicious aroma filling the loch-side air.

'Here we are,' Red grunted in satisfaction.

Her head had started to reel a little, the familiar numbness creeping up her face, the old warning signs that she had never been able to heed.

'No,' she heard her voice like a hollow echo in her head, 'no, I'm honestly not hungry anymore.'

'Och come on,' Red thrust a skewered bird towards her.

She turned her head, 'No really.'

'Okay, but it's going to be your loss, my sweet,' he said, handing Armstrong a bird and settling down to his own. Tina drained her glass and leaned over for the bottle. Jack watched a little anxiously as she poured herself another slug.

'Empty stomach, babes.' Jack warned.

She darted a glance at him, the remark irritated her, she tossed a big gulp back and sat leaning forward, her elbows on her knees staring into the fire. A heavy mood was now taking over from the discomfort of a few minutes ago. The drink was making her deeply morose. She looked across at the two men discussing the plans for the morning. One man, the one that had rescued her from the degradation of the Aberdeen gutters, a man who loved her, a man she had thought she'd loved. She wondered now whether she had subconsciously used him as a mere passport out of the hell she had been living in.

The alcohol was numbing her brain and confusing her reasoning… her whisky sodden thoughts rambled on… she'd longed so much for the dream they both shared. The cottage in Cornwall, marriage perhaps. The loch had come between them and that dream, the loch and its fucking monster and its Charlie's fucking gold. Thank God though, because now she wanted the other man. Big Red Angus, the man she knew must already know her... most probably intimately.

'Where did you get your diving practice?' she could hear Armstrong's voice sounding like it was floating down a long tunnel.

'The Army had a diving unit in Kuala Lumpur. I was one of the team for a while. We were constantly diving for terrorist limpet mines in the harbours. I got my training at the Naval training centre at Portsmouth.'

'It's bloody grim in the loch, I'm warning you.' Jack warned.

'I bet, but don't worry, I'll cope.' Red sounded confident as usual.

She glowered at them both. Evil, destructive impulses goading her, her brain no longer able to control her feelings. Her next words slammed into their conversation like a hammer blow.

'Okay, Red, why don't you own up and tell him you've screwed me?'

Jack had just begun to swallow a mouthful of Glenfiddich. 'Wha...' he spluttered, the burning liquid stopping halfway down his throat and catching on the half-spoken word.

Red Angus sat there, not moving, his eyes on the ground between his knees, unable to believe what he was hearing.

'Come on Red... you have, haven't you... was I good?'

Armstrong was sitting, the glass had fallen from his hand, his lower jaw hung open with the whisky dribbling down it, his eyes red and watering from the choking shock.

'What do you think of that Jack baby?' she shouted, her head was really spinning now, she could see four of them. She wanted to really slash at them now, really slash and stab and turn the knife.

'Fuck knows what he's done to me, but he can do it again

anytime. I fancy you big Red, I've fancied you since the first minute I laid eyes on you. Take me back to your tent and give me what's under that kilt. I'll bet...' She saw one of the four figures get up and loom towards her... then nothing.

CHAPTER SEVEN

The throbbing pain in her head had been gradually bringing her out of sleep. Then as consciousness slowly came, the nausea began to churn in her guts. She belched and the bitterness of bile sprang into her throat. The throbbing grew worse and she opened her eyes. The tent roof was green instead of the familiar brown. She turned her head and stretched her arm to look for the familiar body, but nothing. She groped and found the tubular frame of the camp bed, then found the frame on the other side. Her whisky damaged brain had begun to race to sort things out, panic had begun to claw at her heart. The bed was a single one. She sat bolt upright, the pain in her head excruciating. Realisation came and she tore at her hair in despair, her low moans filling the gloom of the tent. A complete black-out. Alcoholic amnesia, she remembered the doctor's words again. Her last memory of the night before was watching Red Angus prepare the wood pigeons.

'God, God, God, what happened...' she gasped.

She fell back onto the bed, her arms folded across herself, gripping her sides as tightly as she could. She was scared and wanted to vomit. The Aberdeen memories came flooding back. Gradually her right hand moved under the covers, across her breasts and stomach, found the triangle of soft hair, moved down and under as she parted her thighs. No, thank God, no tell tail signs. At least, not that... thank God.

She must have been lying there for another twenty minutes.

She could hear him crunching about on the pebbles, the clanking of metal plates and pans. Then his big shadow fell across the sunlit tent frame. Her heart thumped as the tent flap was flung back and his bearded face and shoulders thrust into the tent.

'Morning.'

She lay there in silence, her hand still on her crotch, she could hear her own heart beating.

'For God's sake what happened?' she begged.

His face began to crease, and he laughed loudly.

'Och, you sure fixed things last night... good and proper.'

'What?'

He stooped into the tent and knelt beside the bed.

'Tell me... for God's sake,' she pleaded.

'You mean you don't remember anything?'

'No... nothing.'

'That's bad, to forget everything like that. Black-out eh, I mighta guessed. I just couldn't understand... you've never shown the slightest sign of recognition, you really can't remember me can you... from before I mean?'

'No,' she whispered.

'Yes, we did screw. In Aberdeen last year... a terrific night. But I don't think I'd have gone through with it if I'd known you were in that kind of state... to think you can't remember. I remember though, it was good.'

'For God's sake, stop it,' she cried out. 'last night, what happened last night?'

'Well you asked me, right out of the blue, to own up and tell Jack that I'd screwed you.'

She gasped as her senses reeled with shock. She clasped her hands over her face in horror as his words tortured her.

'Then you really got going, really into top gear. I thought the poor wee fellow was going to have a coronary. Anyway, you eventually went too far so I stopped you.'

'Stopped me?'

'Yes, knocked you out.' He leaned across to the bedside table and picked up a small mirror and held it over her face. She saw it then, a big shiny blue-black eye.

'Then him and me drank some more, I tried to calm him down, he was pretty broken up. Then he started to get aggressive, swinging punches and all. I didn't hit back, in fact I felt pretty damn sorry for him. He told me to take you back with me... trash.' He called you. So, I said we'd talk in the morning, bade him goodnight, poor bastard, and lugged you into the boat and back here... end of story.'

She let a long deep sigh escape through her fingers, her eyes screwed tightly shut, then she felt his fingers in her hair, gently, so gently running through the strands, touching her scalp, caressing behind her ear. She tensed, her heart pounded, there was a tingling sensation at the nape of her neck that gradually spread down and along her spine. She opened her eyes and saw his face, so near, she felt the warmth of his breath, then he kissed her, his lips gently brushing hers.

'Red Angus!' the shout bounced around the tiny cove.

'Wait,' he whispered, he ducked out of the tent and was gone. He looked up, and there at the stile, halfway up the cliff was Armstrong.

'Can you come up, I want a word,' the voice floated down.

She heard the voice and in that moment she hated Armstrong, her head swimming in confusion and terror.

As Red Angus heaved himself up the last few feet to the stile, he wondered if Armstrong was going to try something, maybe exact some terrible vengeance. He knew that if Armstrong attacked him now, he'd stand no chance. He was out of breath, and Armstrong was above him in a superior position for attack. He hoped his fears were groundless. Then Armstrong's arm was thrust towards him.

'Oh thanks,' grunted Red as he took the offered hand and hauled himself up to the man above. Armstrong leaned back against the stile as Red sank down onto a hummock of grass.

'Look,' he said, 'I don't feel up to much.'

'I suppose you don't,' Red muttered 'look... I'm...'

'Oh, for fuck's sake... I don't want any apologies. You met her before I did, so that's that. It was all getting a bit shitty anyway. If she's happier with you that's good... it's just the way it all happened I suppose. Never seen her like that before.'

'Och, laddie, she's paying for it this morning,' Red forced a chuckle.

'Anyway,' Jack continued, 'I think I'll go into Aberdeen for a few days. Go on the booze with a few of my mates, I think I feel like bit of a binge. I want to get hold of an airlift anyway. I think we'll be needing one once we start diving.'

'So you still want to carry on?' Red asked.

'Oh yeah,' he smirked, 'just like nothing's happened.' They shook hands.

'I'll be gone a few days, then I'll be raring to go. No fucking tart is going to stop me now.'

She'd never ridden pillion before in her life, so the first time on the old Harley Davidson was a terrifying thrill. She clung to him with all her might, her head tight on his back, her heart in her mouth as the 1000cc's roared between her legs. Eventually she learned to cope and thrilled to the speed and the noise and the feel of the man in her arms.

'You okay?' The slipstream whipped his shout away.

'Yeah,' she shouted into the rushing wind.

'Scared?'

'Yeah, but it's fantastic!' She screamed as he dropped down a gear to roar down a steep incline, a precipitous void dropping away on one side, then back into top, gunning the machine again, the speedo quivering at ninety and the vibration enjoyable under her.

He throttled down and she looked over his shoulder at the lone stone and slate building they were approaching, stark against the moorland skyline. The hanging sign told her this was the place he'd mentioned. 'The Clansman'.

'Phew, that was something else!' she gasped, peeling her hair from her face.

'Yeah, she's a beautiful beast.' He said turning off the racket and pulling the machine up onto its stand.

'Crazy,' she said, as they stepped through the door into the tiny bar, 'just like somebody's front room.'

'Bloody sight better than the tourist haunt down on the loch.'

'Yeah, it's nice.'

The furniture was simple, an ancient three-piece suite on a thread-bare rug, and the bar. There were two optics behind the bar, a malt whisky and an ordinary whisky, and one beer pump on the counter.

'Make yourself comfortable.' He said, and she dropped into the softness of a sofa, she looked around the tiny room at the nicotine yellowed wallpaper and the assortment of framed prints hanging on it. Constable's Hay Wain, a 19th century engraving of London's Piccadilly, Tretchikoff's Green Lady, some family photographs taken in the 1930's, a group from a highland regiment, some framed medals and ribbons, and taking pride of place behind the bar above the two optics, a huge print of Landseer's 'Monarch of the Glen'.

Something else caught her eye and she strode over to take a closer look. It was displayed on a couple of nails above the framed medals and ribbons. A honed and wicked looking 18' long machete like knife. She shivered as her gaze moved along the razor-sharp blade to the handle, a carved ivory serpent coiled around and around and entwined at the end through the eyes of a skull.

'God, how evil,' she whispered.

'That's just what it is.' The strange voice directly behind her made her jump and she whirled to look into a face that made her gasp. An ice hard face, the nut-brown skin stretched taut over a bone structure that threatened to split the skin. The thick eyebrows and blond, sun-bleached, cropped hair stood out in contrast to the tanned face.

She winced at the awful disfigurement. Pink, the scar ran lividly downwards from forehead across a sightless white eye to the right-hand corner of his mouth. The face smiled. Not the warm soft, smile of Red Angus, but cold and hard, like a crack in slate. Red walked over, he put his arm around her shoulder. 'This is a very old and dear friend of mine darling. Whitie Frazer meet Tina.'

The crack grew wider and he spoke again, a lilting highland brogue that belied the look of the man. 'Hello Tina.'

'Whitie's been fighting alongside me for many a year now.

How long Whitie?' Red seemed proud, almost showing the man off to her.

'Oh, when was the first time... Aden?'

'Yeah, Aden, the Congo, Biafra.'

The man was short, but she could see the strength in him, he was wiry. Taut and very hard. He reached up to the knife on the wall, fingers encircling the yellowing ivory handle and lifting it deftly off the two nails. He held it across his chest, his other hand stroking the long blade, its honed steel glinting dully in the dim light of the bar.

'Yes, this old panga can tell a terrible story or two. You're right, it is evil... it has committed some evil deeds. But it has its good side too, its been good to me. It has been my companion in battle, and I owe it my life many times over.' Then his one blue eye glinted coldly. 'But it has pointed the way to hell for many an enemy.'

She shivered. Frazer noticed. 'Oh, I'm sorry, I've upset you, come now, what would you both like to drink? I'm the landlord here, can't go frightening away the customers, they're few and far between as it is.'

She shuddered at the thought of drink. The hangover was still with her and she knew the very taste of alcohol would make her throw up.

'Just orange juice and soda please.'

'Orange juice... soda?' Frazer said in mock amazement. Eventually, after rummaging around behind the bar counter, he brought out a very dusty bottle of Britvic orange that seemed to have had a very lengthy shelf life. He served them, Red had his usual big dram, then Frazer disappeared behind the curtain at the back of the bar.

She sipped the long refreshing drink. 'Some friend,' she whispered.

'You're right, some friend. The most dangerous man I have ever known. He's as gentle as a lamb outside of a war, but give him an enemy he's the devil incarnate. I've killed a lot of men, but him… God alone knows. An invaluable mate to have fighting beside you. He's frustrated now, he's trying to settle down and run this pub, but he's so unhappy. His mind isn't here, it's away across the sea in some tropical hell hole. The crackle of gun fire, the stench of death, and the swish of his knife, that's all he lives for.'

'That knife,' she whispered glancing around at it. It seemed to be leering down at her from it's nails. 'Tell me about it.'

Red relaxed into the comfort of his sofa and sipped his whisky with unusual restraint.

'Maybe you don't remember the Congo troubles… you had to be there to believe it. We were all wallowing in the gore. All sides, black, white, mercenary or regular army, were all up to our armpits in the rape and bloodletting. We, that is Whitie and I, were with the white mercenary force fighting alongside Mbutu's army. We'd come across this Catholic mission in the middle of nowhere… I will always remember the sight that greeted us as we drove into that compound. A scene out of hell itself. There had been about twenty nuns, a couple of priests, and a small field hospital dealing with the wounded from all sides. What we found was a compound strewn with the corpses of the twenty nuns, all of whom had been subjected to the most terrible indignities before they were murdered. The two priests were hanging from the rafters in the church, and the patients lying machine gunned and bayoneted in their beds.

There were a couple of villains still mooching about when we barged in… Congolese and swaggering drunk. One of them was happily cutting the throat of a young girl patient, and going about it with gusto when Whitie gave him a burst with the sten. Whitie stepped up to finish him off when the african started a dying speech as his yellow eyes rolled back.

'Take this panga… evil weapon… take it. It will protect you, but it will turn on you, kill you one day, only then will you get to hell, see you there.' He handed the knife to Whitie and begged to be finished off. Whitie duly obliged and cut the man's throat from ear to ear. Somehow, I know he believes that one day the knife will turn on him too. A curse handed down from a Congolese murderer. Black magic is very potent in Africa.'

She shivered again.

'You really love all this don't you? Either that, or you like to frighten me or maybe shock me.' She sipped her drink, holding the glass with both hands.

'It's a pity,' she continued, 'I know there is another side to you, I've seen it, I can see it in your eyes sometimes, a warmth, a gentleness.'

He reached across, his big hand enveloping hers and squeezing gently. 'I'm sorry, I guess there is so much we need to learn about each other, there is so much I want to tell you about me.'

'I want to know about you,' she said, twisting her hand and gripping his tightly, 'I've been wanting to know about you since the first day Jimmy Bell introduced us.'

He suddenly stood up. 'Come, I want to show you so much… tell you so much, come.' He said pulling her arm.

'Where?' she muttered.

'Home, my home, I'm taking you to Skye.'

'Cold?'

'A bit chilly,' she shivered, snuggling inside his encircling arm. They had queued for hours with the rest of the tourist traffic for the ferry to take them across to the famous island. Now they were up on the heaving deck looking into the wind towards the cloud enshrouded peaks of the Cuillin Mountains of Skye.

'Over the sea to Skye,' she said, smiling happily up at him.

'You know, when I was a boy, there was none of this. There was a ferry alright, and just the occasional tourist, but in the main it was just the working islanders. I expect they will build a bridge one day, more and more bloody tourists.'

'When I saw that queue, I thought we would never get on,' she said.

'It's such a bottle neck,' he said, 'there's been talk of opening more terminals, but all that's going to do is attract more tourists, more cars.'

'Isn't this the journey Bonnie Prince Charlie took after the Culloden defeat?'

'Yes, this is it. He sailed from the very spot the ferry terminal is now at, of course, you know what was missing from his baggage.'

'Charlie's Gold.' She smiled.

'Right, the very stuff we're diving for, the stuff we'll soon be laying our hands on.'

'If we don't kill ourselves in the process,' she said.

'Yeah, poor old Charlie Stuart should have had that gold with him, but somehow someone must have slipped it away in the heat of the battle.'

'And started the search for the last 250 odd years.'

'That gold could have changed the course of history, God knows who we'd have sitting on the throne now. It wouldn't be our good Queen, that's for sure. Of course, the clans were wiped out, and the Jacobite cause lost forever. Charlie lost his meal ticket and people have been killing themselves ever since to get their hands on it.'

'As long as we don't kill ourselves for it.'

'Don't you worry lassie.' He said, facing into the wind, beard and hair flowing. Softly the song came from his lips as he watched his Skye looming larger every minute.

'Speed bonny boat, like a bird on the wing,
Onward the sailors cry.
Carry the lad that's born to be King
Over the sea to Skye'

An hour after they made landing, a small green painted sign pointed the way to the edge of the windswept clifftop where the stone steps began working their way down the rocky 500 feet drop to the sea below. They walked to the edge, Red gripping her hand and feeling the gentle resistance. 'Come on silly, it's perfectly safe, a clifftop always looks worse than it is when you actually get to the edge.'

They stood at the top of the steps, the wind howling around them, noisily battering their nylon anoraks and snatching at their hair whipping it into their faces.

The cliff was not sheer, but fell away dramatically amidst giant outcrops, ledges and boulders. They could see the steps going down for about sixty feet then they disappeared into a rock-strewn gully and behind a huge sculpted rock formation to reappear in miniature near the stone quay of a tiny harbour.

He handed her the binoculars and pointed down towards the harbour. 'Look,' he said, guiding the glasses for her along the line of his arm. 'Down there at the bottom of the cliff.'

'I can see the quay, yes, and some fishing boats and nets and things. It's lovely.'

'Can you see the building on the beach?'

She moved the binoculars up past the boats and piles of orange netting, and brightly coloured floats and buoys along the beach up to the base of the cliff. Then she saw it, the corrugated iron of its roof had all but gone, exposing the skeleton of its timbers.

'A ruined fisherman's cottage?'

'Where I was born.' He said drawing her to him. She looked up from the binoculars at him. He was gazing down, she handed him the glasses, he took them but didn't look with them, his arm encircled her more tightly.

'I was married once... a wife and wee boy, seven years old he was. Do you know, he'd be thirty years old next month?' She looked up at him. There were tears in his eyes, tiny rivulets being pushed back over his temples by the teasing wind.

He continued. 'One day they were both out in the bay, she'd taken him to do some fishing, with a new rod I'd bought him. I was away out to sea with the other lads with the nets. It was on the way in... I spotted the oar floating, then the upturned boat. We found them the next day. They were still clinging to each other.'

'Oh my love, I didn't...' She turned to face him, shield him from the wind, wipe his eyes.

'I had spent all my life here,' he wanted to continue, 'I

walked up and down this cliff every day of my life, so did my mother and father. Then after them, the wife and wee bairn. We'd dug out a rough path over the years, but it was always a heavy climb, especially in winter with the wind at hurricane force sometimes and the rocks wet. It's easy for the tourists now, they have a pleasure boat that leaves twice a day from the quay to take them to the islands to see the seals and puffins.'

'Look,' he suddenly said, 'out there,' pointing out to sea.

'What, where?' she said, her eyes searching.

'Gannets, watch.'

She saw the group of about ten big birds wheeling over the waves about 300 yards out.

'Watch,' he shouted into the wind.

'I am,' she shouted back, peeling the hair from her eyes.

Suddenly she saw one of the birds nosedive, then like a giant arrowhead, it's wings folded, it crashed into the sea to emerge a second or two later and flap away.

She focused on the birds, this time with the binoculars, finding it difficult at first to spot them against the foaming sea background.

Then she saw them, picking one out and following its flight as it skimmed low over the wave crests. She could see the big white wings with the black tips. Following the bird, she saw it suddenly rise, hover, then folding its great crescent wings into the arrowhead shape, it plunged into the sea with a huge splash.

'You got one?' Red shouted, his sad thoughts snatched away temporarily by the wind.

'Yeah, one just dived.' Then she saw it emerge slowly, almost with difficulty and struggle into the air, a fish in its beak. She could see it gobbling, it's throat working to swallow, then it flew away, another bird chasing it in the hope of snatching the prize. They watched the birds at their work for a good twenty minutes before continuing down the tiny stone steps.

'This was my home, and my family's home, it was all we knew.' He said, as they stood on the tiny stone quay, the plaintive calls of the sea birds all around them. They were in a natural harbour, the quay nestling in the corner of the cove under the massive cliff. Strangely there was little sound or wind down here, except the gentle lap of a calm sea and the gulls squabbling in their nests on the ledges above. A reef at the entrance of the cove kept out the might of the ocean which they could see spending itself in plumes of white spray on the rocky barrier.

'Come,' he said, taking her hand.

They jumped down onto the small beach. There were no doors or windows on the little cottage, just dry-stone walls including the separating walls of the rooms within.

'Tourists would have done this,' he said, looking at one of the walls which was virtually down. 'These dry-stone walls will stay up forever unless they're torn down. My father built this with his own hands.'

A fireplace at one end of the cottage was intact with its chimney still standing erect and stark as if in defiance of wind, sea and holiday makers. The stone hearth was still there, a poignant reminder of family evenings many years ago. 'My mother sat here many a night, by the driftwood fire, waiting for Dad to come back from the sea.'

'He was a fisherman?'

'Yes, he and five others owned a half dozen boats, they shared everything they caught.'

'Did you go out with them?'

'Och no. He died when I was fourteen. Just too young to go to sea. They were caught in a bad sea one evening. Only two came back. My mother and me struggled on for a couple of years, living on handouts from those who were left and some of the others from a fishing community from the next cove. It was hard. At that age a lad has pride, the worst thing was having to live on handouts. It was then I began to learn to fish. I learned to drift line, hand line, lay nets at low tide, even spear fish. We learned to survive. Then Mum died. It was a tough existence for her, maybe it was the hard work that killed her, or sometimes I wonder if she died of a broken heart... for Dad. She was so in love with him. I buried her out there,' he pointed out to sea, 'just wrapped her in a blanket and tied her to an old anchor and slipped her overboard. She's out there now.'

'Then you met your wife?'

'Yes, very soon after. She came from a fishing community along the coast a mile or two. Then my boy.'

'Oh, my love,' she murmured, holding his hand tightly. 'I knew there was so much more to you, so much more than all that rough talk about killing and cruelty.'

'When they died, a great part of me was destroyed. I had to go on a rampage. The army, then the mercenaries, the world... life itself had to pay for the loss, the hurt. There has been a big empty hole where my heart should have been.'

'No, no more, I want to put your heart back, I want to heal your wounds,' she turned to face him, reaching up and holding his face with both hands. 'Gradually, slowly I will make you happy again, please allow me.'

His great arms encircled her waist and he smiled. 'I allow you. Something always comes out of bad. It was all those years that set me up for now. I don't ever have to work for anyone, to earn a living, not when there's the sea, the loch and the mountains.'

'And Charlie's Gold,' she said.

'Och yes, that'll be nice,' he smiled, 'but God knows what I'll do with the money.'

'No, somehow I can't see you sitting on the beach in the Bahamas sipping Bacardi and coke,' she laughed, 'cos that's the first thing I'll want to be doing.'

'Come on, let's set the tent up,' he said.

'You mean here?'

'Yes, this is where I always camp. Whenever I feel the need to come back here, back to the womb. Besides, it's ideal shelter for a tent, there's the fireplace, it's completely intact including the chimney.'

'Sounds good,' she said.

'At least there's not too much tourist crap,' he said, kicking a couple of empty coke cans, 'sometimes in the height of the holiday season this place is like a rubbish tip, it's sad to see it like that.'

The tide had reached its high by the time the tent was up. He'd erected it over the living room area, opening out onto the hearth and facing the fireplace, in which a glorious driftwood fire was already roaring.

They stood on the wall of the old quay, Red impaling a juicy limpet to the barb of a size six hook.

'Beautifully calm,' he said, 'see there,' he pointed to a spot between two huge rocks at the base of the cliff ten yards out. The swell rose and fell over the boulders, sliding up and down them forming a constant swirling eddy of deep water.

'There's a deep hole under there and a small cave. It's packed with crustacea down there, crabs, limpets, cockles, mussels. A real spot... took a few months to find it.'

'You mean when you were a boy?'

'Yes, when I had to fish for our bellies.'

A deft sideways cast sailed the float across, dropping it in the centre of the eddy. The bright orange bung bobbed, righting itself, then skittered into the flow of the swirl. A minute went by. 'Any second now,' Red whispered.

The line snaked downwards into the deep green sun-dappled underwater world, at first a ravenous blenny darted out of the swaying jungle of foliage, then another. They grabbed at the bait trying in vain to wrench minute pieces away, then a swarm of even more tiny silver fish attacked the limpet in a silver cloud that flashed in the dancing sunlight. Red carefully reeled in the slack in the line as it looped in the breeze. She clung to his arm, eyes glued to the bobbing, whirling float.

The red rimmed eyes of the cuckoo wrasse watched the swinging bait, its red dorsal fin, thorny and erect in anticipation. It moved out from behind the screen of bladder wrack, and the lesser fry of blennies, gobies and rocklings darted back into their crevices. It took the bait scattering the swarm of sand smelt like a silver firework cascade.

'What gorgeous colours,' she said crouching down over the wrasse as it lay on the warm flagstones of the quay, the deep green, reds and yellows of its scales shining in the sun.

He bent down and picked the fish up by its gill covers, then with a quick movement he drew a knife from his belt. He punctured the fish at the anal fin, and with a deft flick he slit the stomach up to the lower jaw.

'Ugh…' Tina squirmed.

She watched, then still holding the fish by the gill, he plunged his hand into the dripping gash, groped for a second then tore out the entrails cleanly and lobbed them into the sea.

'To feed all the little 'uns you've been feeding on all your life,' he said. Then he leaned over the edge of the quay still holding the wrasse and plunged the fish into the water. Pieces of innards, streaks of white membrane and a cloud of scales and blood floated from the still twitching carcass as he plunged it in and out then stood up holding it aloft. 'Clean as a whistle.'

'Doesn't look edible,' she whispered.

'They are not a public favourite, but ok on an open fire.'

That evening they sat on the wall in front of the cottage, where he said the front gate once was, and looked across the bay. The tide was on the ebb and the tops of seaweed had begun to show, breaking the calm surface then disappearing in the swell like the dorsal fins of huge mysterious fish lurking just below the surface.

The dying rays of the western sun slanted across the entrance to the bay, catching the spray from the reef in its pink. The aroma of barbecued fish hung in the still, clear air, and the delicious taste was still with them.

'It's been a wonderful day, what a spot.' She said.

The arguments overhead on the ledges and holes in the cliff face continued as fulmars, terns and shearwaters squabbled over mates, nests, territories, and continued to do so until the setting sun dropped into the far away Atlantic with a usual fiery splash.

They made love for their first time, proper love, not the thing that happened before in Aberdeen. She lay with him and experienced the strength of his passion and the tenderness afterwards. The gentleness that reminded her of that first time she'd noticed the way he handled that pike after cruelly capturing the creature. She lay under him now, the heat from the crackling fire scorching their sweating bodies, her long brown legs entwined around him, totally subdued by this man. She'd given herself; he'd taken, and consumed her. He hadn't known a woman or touched one for longer than he could remember. Now he was sated, now he was whispering, coaxing, gently touching… easing out the hooks, gently, gently. She'd had many men, lots recently, casually, for pleasure, for money, drunkenly… and unconsciously. But none like this man, none like this man she now knew she loved.

CHAPTER EIGHT

They jumped across the stream onto the shingle beach of Red Angus's campsite and he made a quick check to see that nothing had been tampered with. 'I'll make sure the hardware's still safe.' He said clambering onto a ledge and peering into a hole in the cliff face about 12 feet above the ground. He reached in and withdrew a double barrel 12 bore shotgun, a 12 bore single barrel and a .38 service pistol.

'What's this?' Tina asked, unpinning a piece of folded paper from the tent flap. It was a handwritten note. 'Have arrived back. Got airlift, tents, etc. etc. will be in the Culloden Arms every evening till you show up.'

The VW was parked in the pub carpark. There was a tarpaulin covered wooden crate on the car roof and the rear seat was piled high with gear.

'Have a good time?' Tina asked as they sat sipping drinks that Armstrong had bought. Jimmy Bell was sitting in the usual seat at the bar, but they chose a table and chairs in the far corner.

'Yeah, every night with all the boys, you know the story well.'

'Yes, very well.' She said.

'Plenty of booze and clubs. Anyway, I've sorted my mind out now and I'm raring to go.'

'Is that the airlift on the car?' Tina asked.

'Yes, and all fitted up with the outlet to the surface.'

'Good,' Red grunted, speaking for the first time since

they arrived.

'I'd like to get going straight away,' Jack said, 'don't really want to hang around here longer than I need.'

She could sense the feeling in his voice, bitterness, hurt, humiliation, she couldn't be sure which.

'What do you plan to do?' she asked.

'Depends on what we find down there and how much loot we end up with. I still intend to go down to Cornwall and set up some kind of diving cum salvage outfit. But that kind of setup depends on how much money there's going to be.'

'We'll end up with a nice little lot,' Red said quietly, 'but we may have to wait a while for it.'

'You mean treasure trove and all that?' Tina asked.

'The laws here in Scotland differ to those in England,' Jack said, 'ordinarily a find is only declared treasure trove if it can be proven to have just been lost or abandoned, then it is merely classed as lost property and will belong to the owner of the land it was found on or in.'

'What about here in Scotland?'

'Here in Scotland any find is automatically claimed by the Crown.' Tina and Red winced in disappointment.

'No, it's better. You see there's no ifs or buts, the Crown claims it and is bound to pay the finder the full value of the find. So the whole thing is much more cut and dried here. Well, that's the law now, in the 60s, but laws change over the years, so it's now or never.'

'Suppose we kept the whole thing quiet and sold it ourselves?' Tina asked.

'It's not as easy as that,' Angus said, 'where the hell do you reckon you could sell a hoard of 18th century gold coin without questions being asked?'

'What about abroad?'

'That's a possibility, but we'd only get what the going price is on the black market, and there's a good chance that could work out a lot less than we'd get on the legit. Besides, we wouldn't have all that nice publicity, we would be quite famous, real celebrities. Wouldn't it be nice to be able to walk into the museum and look at something that we ourselves had been responsible for? A world-famous exhibit, a priceless treasure, rather than melted down bullion in the hands of some Arab arms dealer.'

'Okay, I'm convinced.' Tina said.

'And me.' Said Armstrong.

'You mentioned tents?' Red enquired.

'Yes,' said Armstrong. 'I think we should camp at Ruthven Jetty during the diving, actually have our base of operation on the spot. I've managed to borrow two big tents from the oil company, and all our other needs for a properly organised professional expedition, we'll do things properly.'

'Good, very bloody good,' said Red enthusiastically, 'we'll need to live on the spot, especially when we start bringing gold up. Don't want those two villains mooching around the site when we're not there. We'll be able to keep a round the clock watch on things.'

'Tell me more about the airlift.' Tina asked.

'It's a kind of vacuum cleaner worked by compressed air. Extremely powerful, it would pick up anything including rocks up to about this size.' He cupped his hands indicating a size about half a football. He took out a pad from a brief case under the table.

'I'll show you.' He quickly and expertly drew the side elevation of the airlift rig in action, illustrating a cross section of loch surface, water depth, loch bottom etc.

'You did that quite expertly.' Red remarked.

'Diving training for oil rig work takes in a great deal of practical draftsmanship. A whole lot of drawing board work.'

'Well your drawing more or less tells it all.'

'I'll go through it anyway. As you see, this is the suction end,' he said pointing with the pencil. 'the rig's got quite a kick to it and it takes a bit of muscle to hold it in place. If the area being hoovered is at all rocky, then beware. If there's a blockage all hell breaks loose, like riding a wild bronco. Lose your grip in that kind of event and the thing is likely to kick your head in.'

'Nice.' Tina smiled.

'The pipe comes up to the surface and through a large rubber ring floatation element, like a big car inner tube. The pipe comes up through the tube and bends back over to face downwards into a large net collection bag. Everything comes up and spews out into the net bag which filters all the goodies from all the crap.'

'Aye, good and simple!' said Red Angus.

'It's not going to filter out rocks,' Tina said. 'if the bottom is rocky, we're going to continually have a bag full of useless and heavy rock to deal with.'

'Let's just wait and see first, we'll cross that bridge when it comes.'

'No point setting up camp at Ruthven immediately.' Tina said.

'Why?' Jack complained impatiently.

'Dive first, make your first recky, see what's down there, then if it looks worth it, all systems go.'

'She's right, woman's logic, there's nothing to lose,' Red agreed.

'It must be very ancient,' Tina said as they climbed up onto the stonework.

The Ruthven Jetty was quite solid for about ten yards from the bank, then it disintegrated as it reached out into the loch, a crumbling edifice to some ancient loch dwelling community, a dying arm of lichen covered, half submerged slabs of stone.

'It's very old indeed,' Red grunted, 'some say it was built about the time that St. Columba was preaching here in the wilderness.'

'Wasn't he the one who was said to have made the first sighting of the monster?' Jack remembered from somewhere.

'Yes, and according to him, that was the first and last time the monster ate anyone.'

Tina laughed, her nose crinkling the freckles, her teeth flashing white in contrast to the gold of her tan. Jack was sitting on a slab of fallen stonework, he watched her, the golden skin, the sun streaked hair, and the lithe jeaned figure. He swore softly to himself, he was going to find it fucking hard to let her go. He glanced at Red Angus as they talked, the bloody big red headed bastard had stolen his woman, they would have made love by now, of course, they would have done... every fucking night, he thought of it, of them together and tried to claw it from his mind, it was making him feel sick.

Red continued.

'The first written records go back to almost fifteen hundred years ago when Adamnan, ninth Bishop of Iona, was writing the biography of St. Columba. He wrote about an incident when Columba was walking along the shore of the loch. Apparently one of his disciples ventured into the water and swam out some distance. Suddenly a great creature with gaping jaws bore down on him and grabbed the struggling man. At that St Columba bellowed at the monster, commanding it to let go at once, which it miraculously did.'

Jack thought at once of the amazing sight of the creature rearing up and grabbing the goose. The thought made him shudder and he felt fear at venturing into the creature's own domain.

'See that rusty pole sticking out of the water there,' Red Angus pointed to the pole which was about thirty yards out, 'well that's the end of the pier. According to what you say, it would have been from there that the Redcoats would have opened fire.'

'How the hell do we get there?' Tina asked.

'It's ok, I've been to the end. The stone slabs are only just below the water surface there. We'll have to get our feet wet, that's all.'

'So long as we keep our powder dry.' Jack said.

'Right,' said Red Angus sitting on the pier, his legs dangling over the edge. 'let's have the musket.'

Armstrong unwrapped it from the oilskin. Tina laid the bag of paper cartridges and wadding beside him.

'This is the famous Brown Bess. The musket most widely used by the English Army of the 18th century.' He loosened the drawstring of the large leather pouch and took out a cylindrical shape wrapped in brown paper. 'This is a cartridge, powder and ball all wrapped in a neat little paper package, hence cartridge paper'

'So, no powder horn?' Jack asked.

'No, too slow in battle, there is an exact measure of powder in this cartridge, enough to prime the pan and the rest to pour down the barrel.' He bit the end of the paper cartridge and a little black powder spilled down his lip and chin, then he poured some in the priming pan, he then dropped the cartridge down the end of the long barrel, he wiped the black powder from his chin with the back of his hand.

'Imagine the state of the poor infantryman's face in battle, they were as black as chimney sweeps.

The range of these muskets varied according to the loading. Two factors dictate range, and these depend on the individual loading the gun. One, the amount of powder poured down the barrel, or the size of the cartridge, and the second, how hard the ramrod is tapped down.'

'So you're saying this musket can't possibly have the same range as the one's that were fired from the end of the jetty?' Armstrong asked irritably.

'Hmmm, these cartridges hold the same weight of powder as the standard army issue of the day. I'm willing to bet I'm within a decent radius. Whatever the case though, we are going to have to search… it's not gonna be easy.'

'You just wait till you get down there, we need anything to make it easy.' Armstrong warned.

Armstrong was taking a strange sadistic pleasure in knowing that once they were under the waters of the loch, he would be the boss. Red Angus was strong and brave, but his diving experience was minimal compared to his own formidable experience.

'Okay, let's be at it then.' Red sighed gruffly. Clearly, he was going to enjoy every minute of this. It was an exciting moment, a re-enactment of a tiny slice of history itself and a real chance of laying hands on that rotting money belt of gold coin nestling somewhere deep amongst the weeds and slime.

'Now get in the boat and wait while I put the first shot over, then for God's sake keep your little eyes on the spot and get over there quickly. The water's like glass so the spot will stay visible for long enough.'

While they waited in the boat, the outboard purring, Red checked the gun again, then promptly dropped his kilt and kicked off his shoes and socks, slung the heavy firearm across his broad back and started hopping from stone to stone. So, they do wear something under their kilts, Armstrong thought as he watched the Scotsman, his powerfully muscled legs lithely stepping then plunging thigh deep as he went out into the loch, walking along the underwater ruin to the half-submerged pole at the end of the pier. Soon, there he was standing by the pole, almost up to his waist. It was a beautifully warm and sunny day, but the water of the loch looked as forbidding as always, as if darkness and danger were lurking just below its tranquil surface. They watched him check the musket again, the priming pan, the flint.

She watched him, looking fierce and rugged, the sun shining in his flowing hair. He lifted the long musket to his shoulder and looked like a throwback to the Jacobite rebellion itself. She shivered a little and imagined being an English infantryman on freezing Culloden Moor that day over 200 years ago, having to stand firm and face a charging, yelling army of wild clansmen all looking like Red Angus. She shivered again.

This was the first time she'd been alone with Armstrong since that horrendous night. She glanced at him, he was gazing down into the bottom of the boat. A twinge of pity or maybe guilt nagged at her and she wished she wasn't there... so near, and alone with him. He glanced up and caught her eye. 'I'm sorry,' she whispered.

His eyes flicked away from hers. 'Look, let's get on with the job in hand.' Anger flared at his temples. She moved away from him along the plank seat. The movement tilted the boat a little just as the hoarse voice bounced over the water surface.

'Alright, me dears!' he was aiming carefully now, in the direction of Urquhart Castle across the loch... the exact direction the clansmen with the gold would have rowed.

'Keep your eyes skinned!' They both tried to focus on the water surface, the approximate area into which they imagined the ball would drop as it lost power. 'Okay now!' the shout came across. A full five seconds ticked by, they could actually hear their watches ticking. The hammer fell, another delay as flint hit, spark ignited primer powder, and a slow low boom as Red's arm and shoulder absorbed the shock of the slow black powder recoil. It seemed seconds... concentrating, searching, then there it was, like a pebble being thrown, a plop then the concentric ripples.

Jack put the boat into full throttle, and they both nearly toppled over backwards.

'Keep your eyes on the spot!' Jack shouted excitedly as the report from the musket reverberated off the mountainous walls of the loch, bouncing off the sides, booming over the water surface, crackling through the pine forests and bouncing back again in all directions across the loch before dying somewhere in the far corners of the Great Glen.

Red Angus stood there and quickly looked around, thankful

this was one of the loneliest places on the loch, with no people about. He was unable to see where his ball was landing because of the great pall of smoke that surrounded him as flocks of water birds, gulls and starlings took to the air in shock.

'Still got it?' Armstrong shouted above the outboard noise. 'Yeah,' she was hanging on to the gunwales as they both stood in the speeding boat. In a matter of seconds, the prow of the little boat was cutting into the outer rings of the dying ripples from the falling musket ball.

'Easy, easy…' Jack muttered to himself, throttling down and gliding into the area.

'Well, this is it.'

'Yep.'

They were idling now. Looking back, they saw Red Angus waving. Jack gave the thumbs up.

'You sure?' came the shout back.

'Wait, shouted Armstrong, just gonna check the depth.' He then lowered the plummet through his fingers, counting off the feet. 'about 40, no problem,' he muttered to himself.

'OK, now it's for real! Red shouted.

'Yeah!' Jack yelled back.

'Okay,' Red shouted.

Moving off again they reached the spot, then retreated five, ten, fifteen yards… then stopped.

'Well, this is it, get the marker ready.'

Holding the plummet in one hand ready to throw, she placed the float end under her foot.

'Okay, ready!' she shouted, crouching down.

Red was aiming again, this time straight at them. He raised his arm in the thumbs up signal again. Two seconds later something hit the water. They both jumped as the delayed sound of the musket boom followed, losing itself once again in its own echoes. Tina flung the weight out and it streaked home into the exact spot trailing the rope with it.

Jack moved the boat quickly to the spot, following the rope as it snaked down plummeting into the depths.

'Couldn't be better,' Armstrong laughed, as the rope stopped playing out. 'yes about 40 feet.'

They both knelt down, their heads over the side, watching the blue nylon rope slowing going down.

'So this is the spot those poor men died,' she murmured wistfully.

'Yeah, give or take a few yards, unless the story in the book is so much bullshit.'

Soon the float was in position, its almost submerged brown top just visible above the surface.

Red was standing on the bank as they edged the boat in, standing hands on hips, kilt back on, looking very satisfied with himself.

'Ok, me darlins,' that was a great piece of work,' he growled, 'the Bonnie Prince must be turning in his grave at this moment. His gold will soon be in our grasp. How deep?'

'Only about 40 feet.' Armstrong replied.

'Ah…' he growled, 'a piece of cake, now let's get the hell outta here, those bangs must have been heard by everybody for miles. There's bound to be police nosing about pretty soon.'

The two figures crouched motionless behind their craggy vantage point 20 yards up the hillside above the jetty, their eyes and ears taking in everything below them.

'Now what the hell dya reckon they're up to?'

'Well, they're either fuckin' mad or they're onto something.' Charlie Barsh hissed.

They watched and listened intently, they heard the last few words of Red Angus. 'Prince Charlie'll turn in his grave, will he?' Loon grunted, a twisted smile contorting his moronic face.

CHAPTER NINE

The cold stillness closed in on them as they ducked under the surface, an immediate contrast to the turbulence and noise above. After the beautiful flat calm conditions of the last few days, the morning had broken in lashing rain with north easterly winds whipping the water surface into two feet waves.

Suddenly Armstrong was in his own element, diving was what he was trained to do, what he was professional at. As they swam downwards along the rope into the darkness, he was aware that here at least he was best, the only time he felt dominant to the Scotsman. He stopped and backed away from the rope, treading water and waiting, looking up to Red Angus as he swam down. He noticed that by no means was the man a novice, but he knew, and he knew Red Angus knew, who the boss was down there.

He waited a little longer till Red neared, then duck diving, he continued down leading the way.

He thought of Tina up there and once again bitterness welled up inside him like bile.

The bottom was very different to the area he had previously gone down to. Here there was no thick vegetation, and none of that putrid heavy slime that hung in almost impenetrable layers. Here the bottom shelved very steeply, at almost 45 degrees, a continuation of the hillside itself. It was covered in scree and rocks, obviously from the hillside. His heart sank. Over two hundred years of gradual land slipping and rock falls would have long buried the clansman and the money belt and put them beyond recovery. He looked up and saw Red still descending and realised suddenly that the visibility was much better than where he had dived before and wondered why.

They had been underwater for half an hour, making a foot by foot search of the sloping bottom as planned. Red Angus moved in ever widening circles, starting from where the weight lay, while Jack swam to a ten yard radius and moved inwards in the same fashion. Another five minutes and they had met in the middle having found nothing. Despondency had seeped into their minds and bodies, together with the awful icy gloom of the place. By the time they had met in the middle, they'd had enough.

Red signalled his feelings with a shrug of his huge shoulders and Armstrong pointed upwards. Together they kicked off from the bottom and let themselves float towards the warm yellow light and the boat.

'Shit.' Red coughed, as he wrenched off his face mask while hanging onto the side of the boat.

'Jees, this is great,' Jack sighed, cupping his mug with both hands. Red Angus sat sipping his quietly, looking morose.

'What's the point,' he grumbled.

'What do you mean?' she asked.

'The bottom's nothing but scree and boulders, that gold must be buried under tons of the bloody stuff.'

'We'll give it ten minutes and I'll go down again,' Jack said, 'I'll finish that other tank. I'll search wider till the air's gone, you never know.'

'Okay,' Red Angus said, 'rather you than me, you're the pro.'

They both sat huddled at opposite ends of the tossing boat. She shrank deeper into her waterproofs, her arms folded and clutching herself, her knees drawn up tightly. She watched Red, huddled in almost the same position. His eyes looked up, meeting hers.

'He's a good diver.'

She nodded.

'He's also a million years younger than me, God, I felt my age down there.'

'This is doing him a lot of good, you know,' she said.

'How's that?'

She shivered, trying to snuggle deeper. She glanced over the side, eyes searching for a couple of seconds, then finding Jack's bubbles on the agitated surface.

'Yes, this is doing him good. It's the first time since we met that he can honestly feel that he can beat you at something. You're bigger, tougher, you can fish, cook, fight better. You don't give a damn about anything or anybody. But down there he can prove to himself, you, me and for that matter anyone in the whole world, that he's tops. He's topping you down there and he's revelling in it.'

'If it makes him happy, great.'

'Oh, for fuck sake,' she said irritably, 'you even took his woman away.'

'Come over here,' he grunted, holding out an outstretched arm. She moved gingerly along, gripping the gunwales tightly. The boat slid into a trough then pitched as it rode the next wave. She lost her grip and fell into him as he grabbed her and drew her into the protection of his encircling arms.

'You glad I took his woman away?'

'…yes, but, the guy's had to put up with a lot.'

'Well, as you say, maybe he's going to get his own back on me down there.'

She looked up at him, the slanting rain bit into her face and she shrunk further into him, pulling the collar of her jacket up over her head, her hands searching under his oilskins and holding him tighter, drawing him closer, feeling his body warmth.

The gaping entrance of the underwater cave opened like a huge and hungry mouth below him. Treading water, he aimed the torch into its blackness, the light exposing the immediate interior. Doubling over, he swam towards the cavernous darkness following the light beam. He hesitated a moment, wondering whether to surface, tell them about the discovery, come down again, perhaps with Red Angus and the security of full air tanks. He decided to investigate a little further. The torch beam bounced off the cave walls exposing a jagged and forbidding interior. Fighting his nerves, he kicked downwards, the cavern mouth closing in on all sides. He glanced at his dial, there was barely a couple of minutes of air left, he'd have to surface. Suddenly he noticed a wall below him, the end, this was not going anywhere, just a shallow hole in the loch floor, he felt a mixed sense of relief and disappointment. A few quick kicks downward pushed him towards the floor, touching its jagged surface. He swept the torch around him for the last time and he suddenly saw it. This was no end to the cave interior, the torch beam had picked up a continuation and he found himself looking along another corridor. The water along this new tunnel was gin clear and the torch beam reached deep along its length. The hole was in fact the entrance to a passageway that turned at a right angle to itself and continued into black infinity.

With his heart thumping with excitement, he turned, looked at his dial and swam for the entrance.

The two men crouching behind the boulder had been watching them since Red Angus and Armstrong had first dived. They continued to watch as Jack surfaced and climbed back into the boat. They strained to listen against the blustering wind but heard nothing but the engine spluttering to life and saw the threesome chug slowly against the wind and along the bank.

'They must have hit on something, dya reckon we should go down and see for ourselves?'

'Na, not yet Loon boy. We'll wait a while and see what they come up with. If nothin' happens in a little while, we'll do somethin.'

'Looks like she's playin' around with both of 'em don't it?'

'Yeah, the dirty little bitch. Obviously, she's not as partial as she acts up to be.' Charlie chuckled.

They spent the lunchtime over a couple of drinks in the Culloden Arms, somehow avoiding having to sit up at the bar with Jimmy Bell. They had decided not to mention a word about anything to anyone from now on.

'By the way, I was amazed to find the water so clear, especially in the main tunnel, why's that?'

'No burn or river nearby,' Red murmured. 'the mountains all around the loch are drained by hundreds of small rivers that pour particles of peat into the water, messing up the visibility. Our good news is that the area we're diving in is not near a river.'

The bright sunshine had them blinking as they stepped outside into the pub forecourt. The weather had changed dramatically and the last of the rain clouds were piling out of the south eastern sky leaving a perfectly sunny day behind.

'The wind has dropped too.' Jack smiled.

'Yep, at least I can sunbathe while you two are down there.'

'If it's topless you're going, watch out for the monster.' Red winked.

'And bird watchers, there are binoculars everywhere.' Jack said.

'Okay, okay, that's convinced me, the bikini top stays on.'

The sunshine had worked a miracle on the underwater visibility. Although clear that morning, it was now as if someone had switched on a light. The visibility had increased at least 25 percent. As soon as the two men had disappeared below the surface, she reached for the clasp on the front of her bikini top and in a split second her breasts sprung eagerly into the warm sunshine, and she looked around her.

'Come on everybody, these tits have missed being shown off, but Nessie, you stay below.' She smirked mischievously and made herself comfortable against the transom.

Together they kicked down along the blue anchor line towards the jagged hole in the loch floor. Armstrong entered the opening first, Red close behind him. They swam down towards the first face, then turned into the tunnel. Their torch beams reached out into the blackness of the cavern ahead as they kicked together into the unknown. Jack continued to lead the way. The peat free water was clear as crystal showing the tunnel walls, jagged and rocky and completely weed free because of the total lack of daylight. They had moved forward about fifty yards, it was at this point that they saw the first skeletal remains.

The bones were strewn all along the tunnel bottom. Skulls, ribcages, limbs and countless smaller bones. They gawped in astonishment as they glided over the corpses. Jack thought sheep, deer, otters, seals, for God's sake, what are they? The normally warm water layer inside his wet suit suddenly felt freezing, fear was gripping him. Something, some predator… big predator. His thoughts flashed to that sight on the loch surface, that great, glistening, muscular neck reaching for the flying goose.

He glanced back, but the Scotsman's torch beam blinded him. He kicked on, the tunnel was opening out in width and he sensed a gradual uphill incline. He guessed that they must have been swimming for about one hundred yards. He looked up and saw his bubbles clinging to the ceiling of the tunnel with nowhere to go to burst. Suddenly the tunnel gave way and opened up into a large open space. Red Angus came through and they both shone their torches around. They were in a natural underwater amphitheatre, an almost perfectly round cavern with a domed ceiling. They swept the sides with their light beams, then both beams met on the opposite side. A jagged black hole. Both men were thinking the same thoughts, the entrance to a lair, some outlandish creature lurking in the darkness, or maybe just an entrance to another tunnel, they tried to calm themselves, to fight the panic that was clawing at their hearts. The cavern was about twenty yards in diameter. Jack wondered how fast this creature of his imagination could move underwater, whether they could outswim it… he thought again of the speed that outstretched neck was travelling. They pointed their torches upward and saw their bubbles wobbling towards the ceiling, then clinging flatly with nowhere to go.

Feeling that Red may have needed a little encouragement he nudged him, then gave him a clear thumbs up signal. The Scotsman coolly took out his mouthpiece and stuck out his tongue. There was no scaring the big bastard he thought. He considered whether they should split up, go in opposite directions, but he sensed danger. This was a terrifying place, his years in the professional diving business had taught him to sense danger when it was imminent and never, never to treat it lightly. He beckoned Red to him.

The sudden explosion of movement and the force of pressure knocked both men backwards in shock. A horrifying split second of a huge greenish flank was instantly blotted out by an eruption of billowing bottom muck that soon filled the cave, rendering them sightless, their torches useless. Again, another surge of pressure, and the terror within both men burst out in a frantic search for each other, shining their torches in each other's faces. Armstrong held up his thumb again… this time no tongue, the Scotsman held up his own, then held out both arms and gripped Jack tightly by the shoulders in a great emotional display of reassurance. They hovered there a few moments, looking back they could still see the billowing disturbance of centuries of bottom residue and faeces still moving slowly towards them like some terrifying sea fog. They watched it billowing, waiting to see if it would begin to subside. Then it happened… for a second the clouds of muck seemed to churn faster… then the great head burst out towards them. A huge slavering visage of gaping mouth, glinting pig-eyes and rows of teeth, then the huge pectoral fins and the thrusting flanks of a huge body. On it rushed towards them, mouth open in a savage snarl, the long body rocketing out from the murk, they could see its dorsal fin raised in fury. That was their last vision of the nightmare creature before they turned and swam for their lives, their shouts of terror bursting in cascades of bubbles from their masks and mouthpieces.

Once around the 90 degree bend they could see natural light above and the boat bottom as they kicked upwards expecting all the time to be grabbed and wrenched down again by that evil maw and those terrifying teeth.

'That was a bloody moray I tell you,' Red insisted, sitting crouched over the campfire, finding it difficult to hold his tumbler of whisky as his whole body continued to be racked with uncontrollable shuddering.

It was now a good forty-five minutes since their encounter with the creature. This was the first time they were using the new campsite at Ruthven Jetty and were all sitting round the campfire huddled in blankets, unable to cope with talking or explaining anything in detail. Jack sat with his mug of tea. He wasn't saying much and was still very much in a state of shock.

'It looked like a moray, but some hellish hybrid.'

Tina had been crying since they surfaced.

'Well, the thing we saw was certainly eel-like,' Red Angus said, 'and it was gigantic. There has always been talk of this loch becoming landlocked from the sea to start with, so why not a version of the moray eel. For God's sake, everybody's been on about the Plesiosaur theory, surely that's wilder than the eel theory.'

'When you think,' Jack felt himself calming down now, the shakes subsiding. 'when you think, a moray does have rather a humpish type of back, so all the hump pictures.'

'Well, what about the long swanlike neck that everybody's photographed?' Red butted in.

'Oh shit, I don't know, all I know is that was the most terrifying experience of my life. I've had sharks in the Gulf and poisonous snakes off the Barrier Reef, and plenty of morays, but for fuck sake, that bastard down there, he's just too much to bear.' He shuddered. 'Honestly, I don't know how I'd cope with that again.'

'So much for dear old harmless Nessie that's never harmed anyone, I wonder how many people have gone missing over the years around this loch.'

'We've got to take stock,' Red muttered, his army experience talking. 'Got to take a break for a few days, have a good think and try and work things out. For God's sake, think of things this way, we've just met the famous Loch Ness Monster in its own lair, we've seen it, almost know what species it is, we're winning!'

'We're winning, when you almost got killed?' Tina said, the tears coming again, 'my God, I think we're now pushing our luck.'

'Anyway,' Red continued, 'this all makes better sense… it's good news about Charlie's Gold, don't you see?'

They both looked at him dumbly.

'I tell you, when I first saw all that rock and scree over the site, stuff that must have built up over hundreds of years of rockslides, I thought, shit, no chance. It would have meant a major excavation job, and then we wouldn't have known where to start.'

'So?' Jack shrugged.

'So this… that clansman was shot and fell overboard with that money bag of gold strapped round him. He would have landed literally on the eel's doorstep. Now what I'm saying is this. If luck's on our side, that creature, well, its 18th century ancestor anyway, would have soon picked up the scent of blood and come out of the cave to find the tasty morsel. So, my guess, and I'm willing to bet my life on it, is that instead of devouring the poor clansman there and then, it would have dragged him back to its lair same as any other animal would, and eaten him there.'

'Yeah, those bones, scattered all over the tunnel and cave floor.' Armstrong said.

'You mean human bones?' Tina shuddered.

'No, wouldn't have thought so. Fish perhaps, seals, maybe even the odd sheep. But Red's right, it stands to reason that the creature would have come out and dragged the corpse down into its cave.'

'There should be at least one set of human bones down there somewhere, and near those bones should be Charlie's Gold.' Red announced, holding up a clenched fist in triumph.

'Say the gold was eaten as well,' Tina suggested, 'after all, it was strapped to the bloke.'

'So? That was two hundred years ago. That eel would have died down there. Most creatures go back to their lairs to die.'

'But it could have shit it out anywhere in the loch,' she giggled.

'Oh shut up,' Red snapped in frustration, 'I don't think the eel would have swallowed the gold. Fish often take inedible items into their mouths by accident, but they always spit them out again. Try it with any pet goldfish.'

'Red's right,' Jack agreed, 'no self-respecting moray eel, or whatever that apparition is down there, is going to knowingly swallow gold. I've seen sharks swallow all kinds of objects, but only when worked up in a frenzy.'

'Anyway, I'm going to get good and bloody drunk tonight.' Red growled.

'Must you?' Tina sighed.

'Yeah, I must.' He said disappearing into the tent. She could hear the familiar sounds of bottles and glasses as she walked slowly away along the jetty.

The dismal interior of the caravan was heavy with the odour of stale clothes and tobacco, the small windows letting in little light and letting out even less of its fetid atmosphere. They sat on a bed playing pontoon for pennies.

'Somethin' musta happened down there,' Loon said, 'the way they came up with all that splutterin' and the bird crying an' all.'

'Yeah, I agree, but we got to bide our time. No use bargin' in and fucking everything up. Either they found Charlie's Gold, or they seen somethin' else. Maybe Nessie gave them a fright.'

'I've been playing around with a little idea though.' Charlie said as he dealt another hand.

'Yeah?' Loon fanned the cards, his face becoming even more sullen as his hand displayed itself.

'What we saw with those two while the boyfriend was below. She's a two-timing little bitch that's for sure.' Charlie said.

'Okay, she most probably screws like a rattle snake, so what?'

'Blackmail, me boy, a little touch of persuasion.' Charlie leered.

Loon Barsh put his useless hand down, 'Now you're talkin' big brother,' he grinned.

It was around eleven o'clock that night. Heavy cloud had built up from the west blocking out most of the twilight. The added cover of the towering hillside and its timbered slopes offered almost complete darkness to the campsite. The two tents glowed from their inner lights, their shadows moving on the canvas. She crawled out into the darkness, her torch beam slicing through the night mist. Her footsteps crunched across the pebbles towards the canvas latrine, then the zip sound of the opening and the zipping down again. The two figures crouched silently on either side of the canvas closet, waiting, listening. The zip again, the torch beam. She felt the vice-grip of the hand on her mouth and smelled its nicotine and tasted its dirt and sweat as the shock numbed her limbs and then her brain, and she slumped into unconsciousness.

The ceiling gradually slid into focus as consciousness came and realisation dawned on her. With the return of her senses came the pain in her arms, they had been twisted behind and tied to the back of the chair.

The imbecile features of Loon Barsh loomed at her like a reflection in the back of a spoon.

'Now, my dirty little tart.'

The realisation of where she was hit her. 'You bastards!' she spat at the face, and the stunning slap resounded in her head as he drew his hand back for the back-hand return.

Charlie gripped his wrist. 'Hang about you idiot.'

'As he was saying, you little slut, we've been watching you and that kilted madman, and we've been wondering what your boyfriend would think of you.'

'Blackmail!' she shrieked with mock laughter. 'God Almighty, you couple of little shits,' and she shrieked again, throwing her head back. She thought of Red, then remembered he would be dead drunk, and she cried out in despair.

Loon grabbed her by the hair, 'Shut up!'

'He knows, he knows…' she was sobbing now. 'Jack knows everything, you got nothing on me!'

Charlie suddenly jumped across, pushing his brother aside, his face a mask of evil. 'Now, what's your secret… what did you find down there?'

'What are you talking about?' she sobbed.

'You were diving, at least your boyfriends were, while you were showing off your tits, what did they find?' he pushed his fist into her cheek.

'Fuck off!' she spat into his face.

'Right, I'll show the little bitch!' His hand grabbed at her jeans front.

'You…' another slap froze her words.

Charlie fumbled unbuttoning her front button, wrenching down the zip. She sat in horror, watching as he pulled at the jeans, lifting her legs high, standing between them. Another backhand slap knocked her head sideways, her ears singing. He pulled off her left boot, then wrenched the left leg of her jeans off her foot.

'No, no!' Loon Barsh started to scream, high pitched and hysterically. 'Charlie, I want to do it, I want to do it!' he was like a small child not getting its way.

Charlie turned to his brother and laughed, 'Okay boy,' he chuckled, 'go to it!

Rape… oh God, she was about to be raped, she dared not scream, terrified of another numbing blow.

Loon stood between her legs. She hadn't bothered about panties when she pulled on her jeans to go to the toilet. She looked up at him, his lunatic face leering down at her spread-eagled nakedness. He was fumbling with his front, his zip. She closed her eyes and felt his rough fingers groping frantically.

Charlie was kneeling behind her head, both hands under her chin forcing her head back, she could feel and smell his heavy rasping breath on her face as he encouraged his brother.

'Go on boy!' and pushed her against Loon's violent struggles.

Loon started moaning… it was over for him, before he started. 'You idiot Loony!'

Oh God, panic thoughts of when she'd last taken her pill… nauseating images of spawning some mentally malformed clone of this animal. She opened her eyes again in time to see Loon Barsh weeping, a thin glistening thread of saliva hanging from his lower lip, dripping onto her belly.

' Oh, thank God!' She realized, and began crying hysterically, her sobs wracking her. Then her guts began to heave, and her sobs were choked by her vomit spewing from her nose and mouth.

Charlie jumped backward, letting go of her head.

'Come on you useless bastard, hold her down… I'll show her a real man.'

He grabbed her face, squeezing it, his fingers pressing through her cheeks, hurting her gums. She cried out in agony and fear.

'I'll show you' Charlie hissed.

Jack saw the last few seconds of that scene as he peered

through the grime of the end window of the caravan. His heart was thumping fit to burst through his chest, the blood pounding in his temples. The woman he loved once, still loved, at their mercy... exposed like that, Loon ravaging her. He fought to stay calm and swore softly to himself. He swore because he hadn't brought his shotgun, and he knew there was at least one in the caravan. All the emotions, the past wounds, the sight through the window, her with her legs up in the air.

Then the rage like a fuse fire reaching gunpowder.

She had just started to blubber the secrets when the door of the caravan burst open.

He had a wooden stave in his hand, his face a mask of blind fury as he crashed through the furniture between him and them.

Charlie Barsh took the first crashing blow across his face. Blood spurted from his fractured nose spraying across the interior and onto the walls as he spun round with the force of impact and crashed into a partition sending everything hanging on it down on top of him.

Loon uttered a funny little moaning sound of fear and Tina began to scream uncontrollably. Then Loon hunched up, his hands on his head as he took his first blow across the spine, a terrible crack... the sound of hard wood on bone.

Jack, face white with uncontrollable anger, steadied himself. 'You fucking bastards.' Then swinging the stave upwards, he caught the crouching Loon in the face. Again, something gave, and blood started to come fast. Charlie was crouched on his knees, his hands clasped on his face as if to control the pain. But his head was clearing and now he was getting up. He stood in the corner, legs astride, arms in a wrestler pose, his face a mask of blood and mucus. Then he sprang, his fifteen stone barging Armstrong backwards across the caravan and into the scuba equipment by the door. Charlie's fists were flashing now, punches thudding into Armstrong's head and face, fingers gouging at his eyes, nose and mouth. Armstrong had lost his weapon and the other Barsh recovering his composure fast was picking it up from the floor. Tina could only watch in horror as the two set about him systematically.

The old Ford Bedford van bumped and crunched to a halt on the pebbles of the campsite at Ruthven Jetty.

He lay there on the floor of the dark van interior, his face in his own blood and vomit. She shivered in a corner, her shock rendering her totally speechless. She could hear the engine switch off, the heavy footsteps on the pebbles, coming around to the back of the van. Then she heard him in the darkness, retching again, then the door opening.

'Come on.' They grabbed him by his legs, dragging him out and letting him drop onto the ground. They reached in for her. She shrank further into her corner.

'Come on darling,' Charlie crawled in after her, 'Oh fuck,' he cursed as he felt the cold slime on the van floor. Then grabbing her ankle, he yanked her onto her back and dragged her across the blood and vomit and out to topple down onto Jack's inert body.

Charlie Barsh knelt down beside them, the moonlight washing his face in an eerie light. 'Can you hear me?' he slapped Jack's face, 'Uh…' he moaned, stirring slightly.

'Can you hear me?' he slapped him again.

'Yes, yes…' he muttered through broken teeth, trying to raise his head off the pebbles.

'Now listen and listen good. If you breathe a word to anybody, the police, anybody, you know what will happen don't yer. Well, we'll leak to the newspapers and every other Tom, Dick and Harry, we know, that you've found something down there. How would you like a million other divers on your patch?'

He grabbed Jack by the hair, pulling his head up. 'You understand?' he wrenched his head up even further. Jack murmured something.

'From now on, you've got a couple more partners boy, we're all in this together now. Tomorrow we'll be over, then I think we all better talk to your ex-bird's boyfriend. If he behaves himself, he can come in on the partnership. We'll talk tomorrow morning.'

'Goodnight darling.' Charlie said bending down and kissing Tina on the cheek. She lay there in the dark, listening to their footsteps going away. She could hear Jack mumbling something, she couldn't catch the words.

'What was that?' she whispered, then realised her speech was back now her tormentors had gone. He murmured again. She moved nearer to him, her face against his. He spoke again. This time she heard him.

'You're not worth it, hell, getting myself half killed, for you.' He started sobbing.

She burst into tears herself, putting her arm around him, pulling herself to him, holding tightly. He moved, the pain making him gasp. She realised what he was trying to do. He was trying to move away from her.

'Get away from me, if only you were out of my life.' He struggled to his feet and stood there for a minute swaying like a drunk, then lurched off towards the water's edge. She could hear him in the darkness, the water noises as he splashed his tortured face, the gasps of pain and shock. 'I'd watch what you tell your big boyfriend,' he gasped in the darkness.

'What do you mean?' The moonlight caught his face as he turned towards her. The sight appalled her, and she instinctively cried out.

The bruising was terrible, and the swellings had misshapen his features horribly, the moonlight making things worse. Dried blood caked the side of his face, despite his attempts at washing, and she could see bits of dried twigs and leaves still stuck to the congealed mass.

She burst out crying loudly, 'I'm sorry, I'm so sorry.'

'Listen…' his voice was harsh, unforgiving. 'Red must not cause any trouble just yet. We must bide our time with those villains, play along with them till we get a chance. Red must not know yet. There's no way we're gonna hide the fact there's been some bother, my face will tell its own story, but for God's sake, no mention of what they did to you. Your lover boy won't take too kindly to that. He'd be likely to blow his cool and blow all our plans too.'

'I'm not sure whether I've got any more plans, if only I had somewhere to go,' she sobbed, 'I want to die.'

'Yeah, maybe you should've stayed in the gutter, it suited you.'

'Shut up,' she screamed at him, then broke down again in fury and self-pity. 'You bastard, I was feeling sorry for you… I was.'

'Go screw with your sympathy,' he grunted and continued to wash himself, cupping the ice-cold water in his hands and splashing his face and head, swearing softly to himself with

159

the pain.

She pulled down her jeans and kicked them off, he looked up and watched her walk down into the water, wading out up to her shoulders.

'What do you think you're doing?'

'You will never know,' she said softly. She winced, almost crying out as the peaty water of Loch Ness stung the tender parts of her body, cleansing her of the Barshes, cauterising her wounds.

She tried to scrub herself, between her legs, her thighs, her breasts, her belly. She sobbed softly, praying for a bristle scrubbing brush, soap, for God's sake! She heard Armstrong walk off along the beach still muttering to himself, full of his own self-pity, no sympathy, no understanding of what had happened to her. She thanked God for the way it was between them now, for finding out before that ridiculous idyllic dream of married life in Cornwall. She wanted to tell Red Angus, blurt everything, then watch him slaughter them like the animals they were. But Red Angus was dead drunk.

Pain, and the claustrophobic heat of the tent with the morning sun on its canvas gradually dragged him out of sleep. He gazed up at the sunlit canvas with the thoughts of last night crowding into his mind. There were sounds outside, the usual camp sounds. He wondered whether the Barshes had returned, how Red Angus was reacting. He prayed the big Scot would keep his cool. He knew the Barshes would force them to talk today. With threats from their shotguns and the even more frightening threats of spilling a story to all and sundry. If the news got out it would all be a disaster. An awful morbid depression weighed down on him as the full realisation of their situation became clear as his mind awakened.

A shadow flickered across the sunlit tent canvas, a butterfly. It flickered again then alighted. He watched the black motionless shape, the beautiful symmetry of its wings. A tear formed, filled his one open eye, then trickled down over his encrusted cheek. The wings trembled a little, as the sound of heavy footsteps on the pebbles came towards the tent, then the shadow flickered away just as Red Angus pulled back the flap and thrust his head inside.

'What the... och! God Almighty, you've sure been worked over laddie.'

'Don't I know it.'

'Come on out... there's bacon and beans if you can face it.'

There was time for them to eat breakfast and talk, before the Barshes arrived. The plan was to go along with them, even tell them about their hopes about the gold. They would wait their chances later. 'Remember, no mention of the eel, if they know, they may be too shit scared to dive, we need to get them down there.' Red grunted angrily.

It was obvious Tina hadn't mentioned that she'd even been touched. Red was behaving much too coolly to have heard the full, horrific story. Armstrong wondered what she had told him.

Tyres crunching on shingle announced the arrival of the brothers Barsh.

Their faces told their own stories of last night's fight.

'Och, you did a good job laddie, I'm proud of you. You came off worst, but you must have given them a little hell.'

Loon's nose and eyes were swollen and blue black. They could see signs of congealed blood in each nostril. Charlie's right eye was non-existent, just a slit and a huge swelling, a plaster sat awkwardly above the bump.

'Alright my friends, we'll get to the point.' They both had shotguns. 'Either you tell us what you've come across down there or we'll tell all and sundry the first cock and bull story we think about, and you'll have the whole world and his wife down to take a look, what dya say?'

Red Angus spoke up. He told them all about their theories about the gold. The dead clansman, the money belt, the cave.

'A far-fetched yarn if ever I've heard one,' Loon Barsh sneered. 'what makes you think that fella and the gold finished up down that hole?' he said, totally unaware of the eel and their theory concerning the clansman actually having been dragged down into the lair.

'Well it's the only theory we've got, old son,' Red shrugged, 'if you don't believe it, piss off and leave us people alone with our dreams.'

'If that stuff actually did go down round about here, it would be covered under tons of rubble, two hundred years of it.'

'You heard what I said, fuck off if you don't like it, we don't mind.'

'No, we're ok thanks, we'll stick it out with you.' Loon laughed.

Red Angus just sat there staring at the ground. It had become clear to him that Armstrong's advice was right. They needed time to plan something, some way to rid themselves of those parasites. Homicidal thoughts continued to play in his mind.

'Okay,' he said suddenly, 'looks like we've got no choice than to count you vultures in on our action. Och, I suppose if we find Charlie's Gold, there will be enough for all of us.'

'Now you're talking Jock.' Charlie smirked.

'No, you listen to me,' Red looked up at them both, 'the next step has got to be planned properly. We've been down there already and there's no point in diving again without a plan. We're going to have to have a good hard think.'

'Yeah,' Jack intervened, 'it's a bloody difficult and dangerous dive.'

'So, go away, we'll let you know when we're ready.' Red added.

'Okay, but remember we'll be watching your every move,' Loon Barsh said, 'any funny business and we'll decide we don't need any partners,' he said, tapping the stock of the 12 bore.

'See yer soon partners!' Charlie laughed as they slouched off along the beach to the van.

The three of them watched the brothers climb into the old Ford and drive up the steep path to the road above.

'The bastards,' Armstrong cursed, 'what can we do, for fuck sake, I've just about had enough, the sooner I'm away from here the better.'

'Okay, okay laddie, calm yourself. We're not sharing anything with anybody.'

'Well let's get it over with as quickly as possible.' Jack looked despondent. 'So there maybe something down there, and I want part of it, therefore we'll have to work together to get it, but I don't relish the thought of spending any more time with you two.'

'Look, come on.' Red cajoled.

'Maybe I'm crying over spilt milk, but I'm pissed off with both of you, and the sooner you get out of my life the better.' Armstrong muttered.

Tina clasped her hands over her ears in an effort to block out the words, but he continued.

'Just let's get on with what we're gonna do and go our separate ways.' She started to cry.

'Who are you crying for? Yourself, me or him?' Jack asked. She looked up at him and wondered whether it was hate or pity she felt.

The sound of a land-rover speeding in their direction, slowing and swerving off the road onto the layby above interrupted things to the relief of all three of them.

'Hey down there,' the familiar blue denim figure of Jimmy Bell stood waving down at them. They all waved back.

'There's a good sighting taking place,' his voice echoed. They could see him pointing towards Urquhart Castle. Looking across the loch towards the ruined tower in the distance they could just see the crowds gathering along the road above the castle. A couple of coaches and many cars had begun a tailback of traffic.

'Just look at that, come on!' Red shouted, and they started to scramble up the foreshore towards the VW.

'Wouldn't it be quicker by boat?' Tina shouted.

'Maybe, but we would have to cut across the area of the sighting.'

'It's a really prolonged sighting.' Bell shouted down excitedly. 'Hundreds of witnesses, it's been basking below the surface for the last hour and breaking surface occasionally, back only, as usual.'

'He'd have an orgasm if he knew what we'd experienced.' Red chuckled.

CHAPTER TEN

They were forced to park about a mile from the castle because of the traffic jams.

'This way,' Bell shouted, 'there's a path... wow, what happened to you Jack?'

'Nothing to worry you Jim boy!' Red grinned.

They followed him over the railing at the roadside and down the steep hillside to a pathway that ran along and slightly downwards. The slight decline made the mile easier than it would have been on the level road and they were soon at the spot halfway down the hillside adjacent to the castle and below the gathering crowds above. Bell pointed, they followed the line of his finger. 'It's just below the surface, the dark shape.'

Jack searched the area with the glasses, Bell offered his binoculars to Tina and standing behind her guided her hands. The morning sun was now on the other side of the loch and shining into their eyes, making things a little difficult. 'Got it,' Jack had connected with the shape, 'I'd be a little cynical if you hadn't said it had already broken surface.'

Tina was searching, 'Where, where?'

Red stood silently, finding it immediately with his naked eye. His many years on the loch had trained his eyes to pick up the slightest change on the water surface. He'd had so many of this kind of distance sightings before.

'That's it okay.' He said quietly.

Tina stamped her foot, 'Where...?'

'Here he comes,' Red exclaimed, just as the crowd above also saw it and a great murmur came from above. Squeals and shouts and a couple of hundred pointing fingers. 'Oh yes!' Tina shrieked as she saw it too.

There had been nothing sudden, just a gradual surfacing of something dark. From where they stood, the portion above water looked like being about a foot high and a yard long. Then suddenly another portion appeared some several feet away from the first portion.

'Humps?' Jack asked just as another shape appeared. The creature just seemed to have floated to the surface almost unknowingly.

'Not necessarily,' Red argued, 'it could be a kind of undulation.' All three of them realised the importance of not mentioning what they knew in front of Bell.

'There's still a whole lot of length underwater,' Tina observed as she studied the long dark shape and the three exposed humplike parts. 'Oh, why doesn't it do something?' Tina urged impatiently.

'Unfortunately, this is typical of most sightings,' Bell said. 'this basking attitude is very common, many fish do just that on warm calm days. Carp tend to do it a lot.'

'What other fish do it?' Tina asked, dying to bring up the subject of eels.

'Oh, most fish I guess.' Bell said.

They watched for a good half hour. The creature sinking and rising and occasionally moving a few yards. Then as they were watching its dark length, it gradually faded from view altogether leaving behind a very excited and happy crowd of sightseers.

Red looked up at the crowd gradually dispersing and the traffic beginning to sort itself out. 'Nobody's ever going to believe them when they get home,' he laughed.

'That was the longest sighting for ages,' Bell said, 'and with so many witnesses.'

Bell left immediately, expecting a busy period at the Bureau headquarters after the mass sighting.

'Tell you what I want to do,' Red Angus said as soon as Bell disappeared over the hill, 'I want to go to that spot in the boat. Just drift around there and watch and wait. We could even hang a bait over the side and see what happens.'

'No,' she cried., 'no way, that's just bloody asking for trouble.'

'Don't worry wee darling, it'll be safe enough, you coming?' Red asked Jack who hadn't said much for a while.

'Yes,' he said sullenly, 'might as well, we'll never be nearer to it than we're gonna be in that cave.'

She sat huddled in the bottom of the boat facing Red at the helm. They'd very carefully and slowly chugged to the spot where the creature had been lying. It was an hour since the sighting. Red cut the engine and he and Jack knelt down and peered into the dark water, Jack with his camera and lenses ready. The water surface was flat and calm, and the boat glided gently into the area. The silence of the loch had descended on them and Armstrong and Tina remembered the first time Red Angus had taken them out onto that formidable expanse of water. The eerie silence, the vastness and the hundreds of feet of dark water under them. They'd only known the Scotsman a few hours. They were both remembering their impression of him during those first few hours, and simultaneously they were both thinking of the destruction he had wreaked on their relationship and their future.

Before setting out onto the loch, Red Angus had gone up into the hillside with a shotgun.

'Won't be a jiffy my loves,' he waved. They heard a couple of echoing shotgun blasts, and within half an hour he had appeared with three large rabbits tied together and hanging from a string on his belt.

'See anything?' Red asked.

'Uh, uh…' Jack said, still hanging over the side of the boat.

'Okay, perhaps old Nessie needs some enticing,' Red whispered as he tied the three rabbits together by the necks, 'now let's make them a mite more appetising,' he gently swung the carcases over the gunwale and picked up a knife. He held the rabbits by their ears, then puncturing each belly, he drew the blade upwards on each, enough for the purplish entrails to spill out and hang down.

'There.' He murmured and lowered the bleeding bundle into the water and played out the rope about twelve feet.

'Now quiet, and we'll wait and see.'

'Ugh…' Tina shuddered, 'you love doing that kind of thing.'

'Sssh…' he whispered, holding two fingers to his lips. 'I'll be doing that to the Barsh brothers as soon as I'm able.'

She shuddered again.

'Shit.' Jack's whisper startled them. He was still leaning over the side peering into the water. 'It was just a movement, a shape, then… there it is, it's massive. Just a dark shape down there.'

Red Angus and Tina looked down.

'Can't see it now,' Jack said, 'the shape… it was long,

definitely eel like, maybe not as big as the thing in the cave, but God its big.'

They waited.

The three rabbits hung motionless, eyes open, all three with their front paws in a begging position, their guts out, in a pink haze of their own blood.

The fish was moving in on them, circling, zigzagging in the depths, homing in on the scent.

'Can't see a bloody thing.'

'Good.' Tina had given up and was sitting in the bottom of the boat. Complete silence again. Five more minutes went by, then... very, very slowly, gently, incredibly the boat was being lifted as if by an unseen giant hand.

'My God!' Tina gasped.

'God Almighty,' Jack whispered. The boat continued to be moved, to be pushed up slowly, easily, then down again, eased down almost.

'What the hell?' Jack whispered, holding onto a gunwale with all his strength. He managed to look over the side. 'It's at the bloody bait... wow, it's huge.'

Red and Tina looked into the water and saw it. It was lying directly under the boat, a huge creature with an enormous ruffled dorsal fin and massive head.

They also noticed the pectoral fins, like no known eel species, they were huge and fan like.

'God, it's got to be a throwback, prehistoric, definitely no ordinary moray or common eel.'

They saw the mouth open as it seemed to tilt the great head slightly sideways, then they saw the teeth. Rows of vicious backwards slanting predator teeth.

'I'd say a much more well-equipped killer than even a moray, a bloody sight bigger as well.' Red gasped.

They felt the tug. 'He's taking.'

The boat tipped slightly, another slight jerk, the sound of something moving against the keel and it was gone. Red hauled up the rope. Tina saw what was on the end and turned away. Just the three heads staring sadly.

They all sat in silence, their faces drained of colour, speechless and listening to their own heartbeats.

'So, how did you do, cameraman?' Red grinned.

'Oh no, oh shit!' Jack fumed.

'That eel, or whatever it is, is going to be a problem down there.' Red broke the silence on the way back to the campsite. 'Charlie's Gold has got itself a bloody hair-raising guardian.'

'Maybe the disturbance we cause down there, what with the noise of the airlift and all, will keep it from venturing out of its hole.' Jack said.

'Maybe… but then maybe not,' Red smiled, 'why don't we put a bait out for it, just outside the hole. We'll wait in the cave and see what happens. Just to see how keen it is, maybe it isn't there all the time.'

'There may even be more than one living in that hole,' she said.

'There may be,' Red agreed, 'the bait could help us find that out.'

'It's as well to find out first, before we start work with the vacuum cleaner, you never know how the thing, or things may react to the noise and vibration. We'd better take bangsticks.'

'What are they?' Tina asked.

'A 12 bore cartridge on the end of a stick, they detonate on impact, like when you ram the end against something, like the head of a shark... or Loch Ness monster.'

'Yes,' she said, 'I remember seeing them on TV once.'

She watched the big bowl of water on the Gaz stove start to steam. Minutes later she was in the makeshift shower compartment, the hot water stinging her skin, the steam, the thick soap lather all over her body. Sheer luxurious heaven after the hell of last night. The tiny chemist shop in a holiday caravan site on the loch-side had all she needed to get rid of every last microcosm of Loon Barsh.

CHAPTER ELEVEN

Three hours later Jack was leading the way down the anchor line again, with Red Angus following with a whole cow's liver tied to a reel and line, no hook.

Jack touched bottom at the tunnel mouth and looked up into the light haze and through his own ascending bubbles at Red Angus and the piece of liver in a shimmering cloud of tiny silver fish. They exchanged thumbs up and entered the hole, their torch beams lighting up the jagged walls. They were relieved to find the main cave empty after their apprehensive advance along the tunnel. Red gestured that he was going to place the liver at the entrance to the hole from which the creature had emerged, and Armstrong gave the okay sign. He wondered whether the Scotsman was feeling his feelings. His heart was pounding, and he could feel the pain of his bruised face and the pulses in his temples under the tight rubber of the face mask. He pointed to the bangstick in Red's hand, and then to his own, trying to reassure him that their weapons would give them a fair chance of retaliation if attacked.

Red laid the liver down, and Armstrong noticed that the little fish were not there anymore, perhaps they hadn't been there since they had first entered the tunnel entrance. He wondered whether they knew and sensed the danger. It suddenly struck him that they had never seen any other form of life in the tunnel or cave, not even the smallest fish.

The liver raised a cloud of matter from the bottom as Red

placed it down in front of the recess.

They retreated, Red playing out the line, not daring to take their eyes from the black crevice, straining to see a tell-tale glint of an eye or a row of needle teeth.

They reached the middle of the cavern, sweeping their torches around them expecting any minute to catch the nightmare vision in the surrounding darkness.

Still facing the creature's lair, they swam backwards towards the entrance. Red nudged Armstrong, gesturing they hide up. He found a recess in the rock wall and backed into it turning off his torch and holding the reel on ratchet so they could hear the screech of the spool if the creature swallowed the liver and tried to retreat into the hole. Jack turned towards the cave wall, searching for his own hiding place. The wall immediately behind him had no holes or recess of any kind so he moved gradually along. About ten feet further along he came to a jutting rock overhang. Feeling his way round the slimy outcrop he discovered the cave wall suddenly gave way into a deep recess overhang with another huge rock above. This would be his hiding place he thought, as he kicked forward into the recess, his torch beam making sure this was no lair for another eel. He pushed himself in, having to crouch down under the overhanging rock. He switched off his torch, then in the blackness he found himself half sitting, half crouching on a round object. He reached under him, scooping the object out and up in front of his face. He clicked on the torch.

He heard his own gasp of shock as the light beam bounced off the greenish visage of a grinning human skull.

He crouched in the darkness, his heart racing. He forced

himself to breathe slower. The clansman, the clansman with Charlie's Gold. He'd been sitting on him. He turned the skull around in his hand and there, at the base, behind where the left ear would be… a round hole, the diameter of a musket ball. He wanted to shout for Red Angus.

Suddenly an explosion of light from the direction of Red Angus. He turned his own beam on and in the direction of the creature's hole. A cloud, just a cloud of muck. The eel had been out. They aimed their beams at the billowing grey cloud. Gradually it settled. The liver was gone.

The sunlight was blinding as they surfaced and lifted their masks. There was another craft tied up to their boat. The rubber inflatable of Loon and Charlie Barsh.

'Mornin,' came the shout.

Red swore under his breath. 'Okay now,' he whispered out of breath to Armstrong. 'Play it cool, remember.'

'Look what I got,' Jack gasped in a whisper.

'Wha…'

Jack lifted the skull out of the water, his back to the two boats to shield his find.

Red gasped and grinned. 'Ssssh… not a word.' They kicked the few yards to the boat and pulled themselves aboard. Armstrong dropped the skull under the seat planking unnoticed. Tina, her face tense and drained of colour, sat with her hands between her knees.

'You okay?' Red asked, putting his hand on her knee, 'anything happen?'

'No, I'm okay,' she said.

'We thought we made it clear.' Charlie Barsh rasped, aiming

174

his double barrel shot gun at them.

'Take that gun off me.' Red growled.

'We said this thing was going to take a little planning. We went down for a little recky, that's all.' Jack said, trying to cool the situation.

'Well, what did you find?'

'Nothing, yet,' Jack replied, 'we'll start tomorrow.'

'Be here sharp at ten. But be warned, bring your equipment and your guts with you.' Red sneered.

'Who fancies a drink?' Red asked as soon as the Barshes were out of earshot. 'We've gotta talk about this laddie's find.'

'Yeah,' Jack turned to Tina triumphantly, 'the clansman with the gold, I found him.'

'What…'

'Yeah, his skull, complete with bullet hole.'

Red put his arm around Armstrong and hugged him. 'This really calls for a drink.'

Jack reached under the boat seat and lifted out the skull and tossed it to Red Angus. Red caught it with both hands, turned it round, and poked his finger through the hole with a chuckle. Then he turned it around in his hands again, holding it the way he would hold the face of a beautiful woman, then kissed it full on the grinning mouth. For some reason the teeth and lower jaw were still attached by a membrane of sorts, so the skull really grinned.

Red Angus and Tina spent the evening in the desolate pub on the moor, the pub of Whitie Frazer, that disturbing little man that Red called a friend.

They talked and drank well into the early hours of the

following morning, Whitie Frazer joining in on the drunken, happy evening. Before they stepped out into the moorland night, Red turned to Frazer. 'Listen my friend, we might be needing you soon.' The hard little face creased into a mischievous grin.

'Anytime, just give me the nod, you know that... anything interesting?'

'Yes, very, just up your street, we're expecting a bit of bother, but it may be something we can handle ourselves.'

'I'm away in Aberdeen for awhile,' Whitie grinned. 'I'll look you up when I get back. Ruthven Jetty you said?'

'Yes, see you soon old mate, we'll be there.'

Tina wondered whether Frazer would be bringing his panga when he came. She shuddered and snuggled deep into her coat. She gazed into the dark distance, at the mountains moving starkly against a purple sky as their car sped home along the lonely moorland road.

CHAPTER TWELVE

She rubbed a hole in the misted up window of the car and peered out across the grey waves to the man huddled in the boat. The man was Charlie Barsh. Her two men were below with the other brother, Loon. About three yards from the boat she could see the float of the airlift outlet pipe bobbing and shuddering amid a turbulent mass of bubbles and spewed up bottom muck. She imagined them down there and had worked out from their description of the tunnel and cave that they would be somewhere under the jetty on which the car was parked.

Loon Barsh had managed the descent all the way into the main cave very well. They had expected a possible reluctance, even a change of heart from him once they were in the tunnel, particularly after the right-angle bend. Both Red Angus and Armstrong were disheartened by the obvious determination of the man.

The airlift was working perfectly. Armstrong was standing legs astride and knees bent to help absorb the shocking vibration of the machine as it devoured the cave bottom with a rattling, whooshing noise. They'd noticed immediately that it was not impairing the visibility, but in the act of disturbing the centuries of bottom residue, the stench of rotting animal and vegetable matter was appalling.

While Jack worked, Red watched the entrance to the creature's lair, always expecting a rushing attack. He had his bangstick and the weapon gave him some feeling of security. Jack had his dangling from a loop on his wrist, and Loon Barsh hovered at the cave entrance with a big pneumatically powered harpoon poised, as a frightener for Jack and Red Angus, being blissfully unaware of the terrifying creature in the hole.

They had decided they would start the airlifting from dead centre of the cave and work outwards in circles. This way they wouldn't miss a square inch of the bottom. But first they searched the recess in which Armstrong had found the skull. They vacuumed the hole down to clean rock and found nothing. Then they moved into the centre of the cave and started the main search.

An hour went by, Armstrong was now feeling tired and cold. The machine was beginning to jar his senses, his hands and arms were beginning to go numb. He was experiencing a sickening pain in his head and the sinus cavities behind his nose and ears were starting to protest… he was tasting blood. Red Angus, too, had started to feel the cold creeping into his very soul and pain was gnawing at the joints of his arms and legs. He looked across at Barsh. He had given up his standing posture at the cave entrance and was now crouched on the cave floor, the harpoon on his knees. Red looked at Armstrong. He figured he must have covered a circular area, a diameter of approximately twenty feet and wondered what the net on the surface was filling up like. Suddenly the dull ache behind his eyes increased and he could feel the cold starting to clamp down and his body heat drain.

He kicked towards Armstrong, his eyes still on the eel entrance. He swam awkwardly, his kicking erratic and inefficient. He tapped Armstrong's shoulder, but there was no response. He tapped again, then shoved him. Armstrong looked round, and Red gestured to the surface, grabbing him by the arm and pulling. The racket of the airlift suddenly died as Jack switched it off and an eerie silence fell upon them. Red gave the thumbs up okay sign, and Armstrong returned it, dropping the machine and kicking off towards the cave entrance and into the tunnel. First him, then Loon Barsh. Red turned to look back and saw a movement in the crevice, a water disturbance and something dark withdrawing into the hole. He waited, then a movement again and the big head emerged, the mouth working with the gills and pig eyes shining in the torch beam. Fear gripped him, the pain in his sinuses increasing as his temples pounded with his heartbeats. He switched off his light, and turned his back on the darkness, kicking towards the distant lights of the other two men.

Surfacing and hauling themselves into the boat in their exhaustion was an ordeal of cold and pain. It was a full hour wrapped in blankets and huddled around the brazier with mugs of hot tea before the pain and shivering cold subsided.

'Okay, let's go get the net.' Charlie Barsh said. It was still attached to the outlet pipe on the surface.

'Could you see anything going in?' Red asked

'No,' Charlie said, 'too much water disturbance, but hell, the bleedin' stink.'

'Yeah, it was bad down there too,' Jack said wearily.

Tina sat watching all four men. Wondering despairingly how on earth they could rid themselves of the two brothers. Loon still sat huddled and shaking, not speaking.

'What's up laddie?' Red asked, 'too much for you was it?'

'Cold as fuck down there…' Loon mumbled.

Red laughed, 'You've taken on a man's job now sonny, don't forget that.'

'Oh, go screw yourself!' Loon shouted.

It was 2pm before they'd piled the contents of the net onto a ten foot square piece of tarpaulin laid out on the flagstones of the jetty. The grey skies of the morning had broken, and a hot mid-day sun had begun to scorch and dry the banks and hillsides of the Great Glen. The boulders and the heather, the reed margins and the warming water surface gently steamed in the warmth of the day's changing mood.

'Hell, the sun's strong,' Jack said.

'Good, it'll help dry this pile,' Red said kneeling beside the mass of oddly shaped lumps caked in an evil smelling green grey clay-like substance.

'It would be better to hose it down while it's still wet.'

'We've got a pump and hose,' Charlie Barsh said, 'I'll go get it.'

Thirty minutes later Charlie was standing up to his knees in the loch working a hand pump while Red Angus aimed the hose at the stinking haul. The muck fell away under the powerful stream of water, while Armstrong brushed away the more stubborn lumps.

'Bones,' Tina exclaimed, 'masses of bones.'

'I thought so,' Red Angus said. 'there have been eels down there since time began. There had to be plenty of skeletal remains.'

'Eels?' Loon Barsh queried.

'Yeah, common eels, but big, there are millions in the loch.'

'Eel bones?' Tina asked.

'Some of it must be, I suppose these eels would have been going back to that cave to die for centuries. Remains of food as well I suppose, hence a fish head,' he said, picking up a fish skull and hosing it.

'Salmon.'

'Yeah, or large trout. A pike's skull is much more shovel-like, there's bound to be a few of those.'

'Balls to bloody fish bones, what about some gold coins?' Loon complained.

'Now this would have been an odd looking fish,' Red mused, picking up a bone.

Loon had walked over to take over the pumping from Charlie.

'Human?' Tina whispered.

'Looks like part of an upper arm, too small for a leg.'

'Could be a child's leg,' Tina said.

'No,' Red Angus whispered hoarsely 'we mustn't start kidding ourselves that these eels actually prey on humans. The dead clansman with the gold, okay, but only because he fell in and sank onto the creature's doorstep and was dragged into the cave, yeah, I wouldn't mind betting that this is human, it'll be part of the skeleton that belongs to that skull.'

Charlie Barsh had begun to saunter across the jetty towards them.

'Sssh now, we don't want them to know about human remains.'

'If these are part of the remains of the clansman, then we really are onto the gold,' Tina whispered excitedly just as Charlie Barsh walked up. 'Any gold?' he asked, stooping down to look at the pile.

It took them three hours to clean off all the objects in the pile. Eventually they were gazing down at the cleaned up haul.

A large pile of assorted fish bones and skulls of salmon, trout, and various size pike heads. The rest of the pile was made up of stones and rocks of various sizes.

'Not one blasted piece of gold.' Armstrong muttered.

'Reckoned all along you were talking bullshit,' Charlie scoffed. 'Hey Loon, there's fuck all here, not a single gold coin, not even a brass farthing, why the hell should there be gold in a cave anyway?'

Red glared up at the sneering man, 'Look, you've been told before, if you don't believe in what we're doing, then the best thing for you to do is bugger off.'

'You're fuckin' mad, you are, all three of yer.'

'Disappointed?' she asked him, as they lay together in the tent.

'Yes, I suppose so. It would have been nice to have found something, anything to prove we are on the right track, anything to compensate for the utter misery of that hole down there. I saw that eel again,' he suddenly said, then he cursed himself for having mentioned it.

She sat up. 'Oh no what did you see?'

'While we were getting out of the cave, I turned to have a last look and there it was, just disappearing into the hole, that's all. I suppose the vibrations and the racket of the airlift kept it well hidden, but the moment we switched off, it poked it's ugly snout out to see what all the din was about. I didn't tell Jack, it's scary enough down there.'

'I suppose there's a certain amount of comfort in the knowledge that you may be safe so long as that airlift is working. Its sheer agony having to wait on the surface knowing you're down there with that monster and one of those scum with a harpoon.'

'I told you before, we'll sort those two villains out. I just don't want to get in any rough stuff right now we're on the verge of a find. You never can tell with violence of any kind, no matter how well planned, things can go wrong, don't let's tempt fate before we've even found the gold, imagine if things got screwed up somehow and the police got involved or something, we'd blow the whole thing before we even got started. Besides, there may not be any gold down there, in which case there's no need to worry about trouble.'

'I suppose I understand,' she said settling down and drawing her knee up over his thighs.

'Believe me girl, I know, when violence erupts, it erupts in all kinds of goddamned unpredictable ways.'

Jack lay alone in the darkness of his tent. It was two hours since he turned in, but sleep was still escaping him. He could just hear the low murmur of their voices. The deep sounds of Red's voice and the softer higher sounds of Tina. His mind was still filled with thoughts of the day, the awful terrifying presence living there. He reached up to his face and gently touched the tender bruised areas around his eyes and nose and thought again of the Barsh brothers and how, if ever, would they get rid of them. He wondered how he'd cope if and when the time came, and they were forced to fight them or even kill them. Red Angus had killed many times before and seemed to enjoy the prospect. He'd have to let him lead the way, decide when and where.

He thought again about the creature, wondered whether the reason they hadn't seen it was because it had been frightened and hiding from the noise of the airlift. He knew that certain predatory fish were attracted to noise and vibration, remembering his experience with sharks in the Gulf of Mexico and the Gulf Straits of the Middle East. He remembered the day five years ago, a day etched blood red on his memory. Abadan, there were twenty divers working when there was an explosion. No one was killed, but ten minutes later during the emergency repair work sharks appeared. The vibration from the explosion had brought makos, hammerheads, blues and whites from all directions. There was a mass frenzied attack. He remembered the calm blue water boiling and frothing and changing colour as the blunt triangular fins scythed in. He remembered the nightmare visions of jaws and teeth. The screams and the sounds of crunching and the shuddering bodies as they were torn apart and fought over. The rescue copters were soon on the spot and ten of the twenty were scooped to safety. He had been one of the ten.

There had been countless instances during the big sea battles in the pacific, when sharks would move in on helpless survivors, attracted by the vibration of battle, and the explosions of sinking ships.

He thought again about their amazing discovery of the last few days. They'd found and seen the world-famous Loch Ness Monster. They had found it in it's own lair and could take anyone brave enough to see it if proof were needed. They had discovered it was no plesiosaur, but a fish, an eel, a prehistoric cousin to the moray.

This was a major scientific discovery, one that would startle the world, ram all the clap trap back down the throats of the cynics. Then, even more amazing still was the almost certain fact that they were on the verge of finding Charlie's Gold. The world-famous lost treasure itself had, with such incredible coincidence, led them to the very lair of the equally famous creature of the loch. Then again that horrific vision of the attempted rape forced its way into his thoughts, that frantic vision of Loon Barsh, the drooling mouth… his woman… oh God.

Gradually his thoughts of lost treasure and monsters and evil men, and man-eating sharks, began to slip and slide in and out of focus, and he lapsed into the even more surreal world of sleep at last.

CHAPTER THIRTEEN

Red Angus aimed his torch beam upwards. Their air bubbles had accumulated to form three huge pockets of used air trapped in the domed ceiling of the cave. He watched Jack's and the other man's bubbles rising to join the trapped air, and he wondered what would happen if they used their scuba tanks long enough. Eventually the cave would fill with air and force all the water out through the tunnel. Then he thought of the immense water pressure from the loch, and he decided he didn't know what would happen. His mind had begun to wander for the last fifteen minutes. Armstrong had been working the airlift for an hour and once again the agonising cold had seeped through to Red Angus's very soul and a terrible melancholy had overcome him. Thoughts of the monster fish had begun to panic him, and he wondered how the other men were feeling.

Again, he was impressed with the staying power of the Barshes. This time it was the turn of Charlie and he seemed to be coping even better than his brother. He hovered in the middle of the cave, alert at all times, the harpoon a constant menace.

Always aware of the dark crevice at the periphery of his torch beam, Red thought of that slavering head sliding out and panic churned his guts. He tried to think of something else, and looked away from the hole and saw the black entrance to the tunnel and the thought came to him again… suppose the creature was out in the loch at the time they came into the cave, and suppose it arrived back in the middle of everything.

He sensed that his mind was beginning to play games again and knew that the others must also have had enough. It was time to quit for the day.

The airlift turned off left almost complete silence except for the air bubbles. Again, he watched the hole on the way out, and there it was again... a movement, a cloud of muck as something began to emerge. He switched off his light and turned into the tunnel, kicking like hell.

The warm upper layers of the loch were pure ecstasy as they slowly floated upwards from the cold depths into the sun.

'Still no bloody nothing.' Jack cursed as he poked carefully in the pile of steaming muck on the tarpaulin. 'Well, you can just keep graftin' till you come up with somethin'. Loon Barsh said sullenly.

'If you ask me, they're loonies, fuckin' gold my arse,' Charlie added. 'come on, tell us, what the fuck would the gold be doing in the cave. Who put it there?'

'Shut up sonny, we don't have to explain anything.' Red growled.

'Hey,' Jack was peering closely at something in his hand. 'Look what I found.'

The two Barshes rushed forward dropping to their knees.

'What is it, a coin?'

'No,' Jack said, 'but things are looking up,' he held out an open palm. It was a black object, about half an inch across, a battered round shape with a flattened side to it.

'A musket ball.' Red Angus murmured.

'Yep.' Armstrong tossed it into the Scotsman's hand.

Red rolled it in his palm, and winked at them and whispered, as Barsh wandered off, 'The gold's got to come soon my wee bairns.'

'Let's see,' Tina said, taking the ball from Red.

'That flattened side is where it came into contact with our clansman's skull,' Jack said.

'Okay, okay, keep lookin.' Loon strode over, levelling his shotgun.

Another half an hour went by and they continued to painstakingly pick through the last of what was left. Then Tina picked up what looked like a flat stone covered in moss and slime. She squeezed it between her thumb and forefinger and slid her thumb across the hard smooth surface underneath. The pure, clean gold gleamed in the sun.

They all heard her gasp.

'Yes,' Red breathed, 'It looks like a Double Louis d'or, Louis XIII, minted in 1643.'

'Shit...' Jack sighed, 'God, we've done it, we've bloody done it.'

'Right oh,' Loon Barsh snarled, grabbing at Red's hand. 'We'll take care of that.'

Red pulled his hand away and stood up. 'No, you won't, you scrounging bastards.'

'Oh yeah, we will,' Charlie smiled pushing the safety catch forward on his shotgun to emphasise the words.

'We'll take care of all gold coins you find until you've raised the lot, then we'll divvy up.'

Red stood up and backed off to the edge of the pier, his knuckles white and clenched round the coin.

'Let them have it!' Tina pleaded.

'Yeah, I'll let them have it okay!' Red shouted.

'Please darling!' Tina begged.

'Okay, we'll let you have your way, but every last coin that comes up will be counted, and God help you if you try any funny business.' Jack said stepping across to Red and taking the coin from him.

'You can have it when we pack up today, when we've finished going through what's left.'

A half hour later they were finished. Three more glittering Double Louis d'ors lay on a bed of Kleenex tissue on the flagstones.

'See you tomorrow then,' the Barshes waved, the precious bundle of Kleenex snugly in one of their pockets.

'Remember to keep them away from each other, keep the tissue between each,' Red warned, 'they're mint condition coins.'

They watched the two walk up the hillside. They waited, standing silently, forlornly on the jetty and heard the car engine start and drive north on the Foyers Road back to the Barsh caravan.

'Shit,' Tina spat out.

'They must be laughing their filthy heads off.' Jack sighed.

'Och… don't worry laddie,' Red smiled, 'we'll have the last laugh, you'll see! The time has come to plan the Barsh brother's departure, departure from this world.'

'Oh God,' Tina shuddered.

'Come now,' he said, 'we've got some celebrating to do, we've found Charlie's Gold!'

He put his arms round Tina and Jack and crushed them in a huge bear hug. 'We're gonna have a wee drink on that.'

After a few large tumblers of Glenfiddich sitting around the brazier, the alcohol began its mellowing effect.

'Amazing what a couple of drinks will do,' Jack said warming his drink over the red hot coals, 'things don't seem half as bad now.'

'I know what you mean,' Tina smiled, 'I was all ready to suggest calling the police or something just as crazy.'

'No, no, no...' Red growled, 'we're going to make our move now... now is the time!'

'This is what we'll do,' Red spoke quietly, moving forward on the edge of his chair. 'There's no way out now, these two won't let go easily,' he paused for a few seconds, took another slug from his glass, then looked at them both intently, 'we're going to have to kill them, I'll do the actual topping, but you're going to have to help me.'

Tina shuddered, tears welling in her eyes, Jack's heart pounded, the whisky not supporting him as his courage drained.

Red continued, 'we'll do it in the cave, that way there's absolutely no problem about getting rid of the corpses.'

Tina looked at him, her eyes filled with horror, her stomach churning with nausea.

'We'll go down tomorrow as normal,' Red looked at Jack, 'you start airlifting and leave the rest to me.'

'You gonna cut their air pipes?'

'Yes, it's the only way, there are other ways in normal circumstances, but we can't take a chance with blood in the water, not with that eel. I'll cut his air pipe and his automatic reaction will be to go up, make an ascent. He'll hit the ceiling of the cave, and that's where he'll die. Then it will be his brother's turn.'

'But he'll panic, he'll come after our air, he'll be going berserk.'

'No, not in that cave,' Red smiled, 'we'll switch off our lights, his disorientation will be total, no chance. We'll tell the other one that his brother was too weak to make the ascent, that we need to dive again, this time needing his help. Then the same applies,' he said grinning and running his finger across his throat. 'Then we continue to harvest the gold at our leisure and leave them down there as eel fodder. Their bones will stay down there for all eternity.'

'Simple,' Tina said, 'nauseatingly simple.'

'No time for qualms now darling, we're actually there, nothing, absolutely nothing must stand in our way now.'

'By the way, you seem pretty knowledgeable about gold coins?' Tina said.

'Oh, I've read a few books, got a couple at the camp on the other side. I've lived on this loch a long time, and I've lived with the legend of Charlie's Gold for too long not to have done a bit of reading up.'

'Those coins were beautiful,' Tina sighed, 'so big and shiny, just beautiful.'

'Plenty more where they came from my dear!' Red winked.

Dawn broke as it did on the day before, under a cloudless sky, the eastern horizon a glow of pinky orange over the hills. Tina wondered what the day had in store for them as she watched Red kneeling at the water's edge cleaning his teeth. Jack lay in his tent, sleep hadn't come easily all night, and the little that had come had been fitful and dream filled. He lay on his back looking at the lightening canvas. Visions of the two dead brothers in wet suits hanging lifeless, with sightless eyes staring down haunted his subconscious. The sickness in his stomach, the sickness of fear hadn't subsided since he had crawled out of the tent at 2am and spewed onto the pebbles. He prayed, for himself, for Tina and Red Angus, and he prayed that his courage would hold up when he most needed it.

Tina sat in the Volkswagen on the quay. She watched the three men roll backwards into the glass calm loch and whispered a prayer.

Armstrong switched on the airlift and it hummed into life. He watched the green residue on the cave bottom sliding towards the mouth of the pipe and disappearing,.'

Unseen objects rattled up the pipe and up and away along the tubing. He pretended total concentration, his heart in his mouth, his breathing fast. He was aware of his breathing, worried that the quickness of his exhaling would give the alarm. Charlie Barsh hovered by the entrance, alert, the harpoon always menacing. Red had said he would bide his time, maybe wait till the end of the dive when Barsh was exhausted. A good half hour went by and it seemed like a lifetime. Then Red moved. Jack could feel the pulse in his temple, pounding painfully under the rubber of his mask. Red Angus couldn't afford to fluff it, that harpoon would cause horrendous damage. He watched Red move towards Barsh. Red began to gesture something, making signs with his hands. Barsh moved there, Red gestured again, an ambiguous motion with his hands, Barsh backed off a little, perhaps sensing danger. Then Red made his move. Jack saw the quickness of his hands, the glint of torchlight on his knife and the burst of bubbles from the severed air hose.

Red saw the horror filled eyes in close-up before they were engulfed in bubbles. He backed off as Barsh flailed in panic then kicked upwards and into the huge flat air bubble on the cave ceiling, his air tanks clunking on the jagged rock. Barsh struggled, eyes wide, mouth gulping, his hands clawing at the trapped air pockets as they split and moved, sliding away to form separate bubbles that rolled away from the turmoil. Then Barsh must have gathered his thoughts, he was suddenly jack-knifing, diving downwards again. Armstrong backed away, still holding the airlift. He saw the flailing figure kicking desperately towards him, hands clawing for his face, for his mouthpiece.

Instinctively he kicked backwards bringing the airlift tube upwards and crashing it into Barsh's face mask shattering the glass and knocking it upwards off his face. The stunning impact of the tube halted the frenzied bid for his air, and again the threshing figure floated upwards to the cave ceiling. They watched his struggles, the vain attempts to gulp the air from the bubbles on the ceiling, the desperate attempts to mouth the severed air hose and the gradually weakening struggles of death. Within three minutes he was dead, the still twitching corpse hanging lifeless from the ceiling, face mask askew, eyes staring down at them accusingly, mouth gaping since its last desperate gulp for air.

Red swam across to Armstrong, holding him by the shoulders. Jack could see his bulging cheeks, his jubilant grin and he heard his triumphant shout as bubbles exploded from his mouthpiece and mask. He shouted back, both thumbs up in a victory salute.

They continued to work for another 15 minutes. For the first time they heard a new sound in the airlift tube. The rattling sound of hundreds of metallic objects.

Then they surfaced.

'Barsh!' Red Angus spluttered, 'Get your tanks on fast, your brother needs help, he couldn't make it to the surface, we gotta get down to him!'

'Wha… Oh God!'

Within a couple of minutes Red Angus, Armstrong and Loon Barsh were heading back down the guide rope.

Jack led the way into the main cave, his torch beam aimed downwards and away from the grotesquely contorted hanging corpse. He had half expected the body to have floated down to the cave floor, but there must still have been air in poor Charlie's lungs, his last gulp for life. They swam into the middle of the cave and Loon looked round urgently. Red moved up behind him. Light ricocheted around the cave as Red dropped his torch to dangle from his wrist as he ripped Loon's face mask upwards and off his face while his left hand came up with the knife.

Armstrong spun round, aiming his torch and caught the image in his beam. Loon's face a mask of terror amidst a cascade of bubbles. He switched off, backing away in the darkness. They heard the desperate underwater gurgling cries, the clunking of air tanks against the rocks, the spewing of wasted air. Red switched his light on. The brothers were together on the ceiling. Loon grabbing at his brother's corpse, wrenching at the dead man's air hose. Both figures seemed to be enveloped in the huge bubbles of carbon dioxide and compressed air.

Armstrong wondered for a moment whether Loon could survive in the now huge bubble, swelled even bigger by the severed air hoses. He seemed to be totally encased in the bubble, his mouth sucking in air and water, his hands clawing. They realised that he was surviving, they could see him breathing normally now, looking down at them.

Red Angus grabbed the airlift. Swimming upwards he pointed the intake at the air pocket and switched on. Loon's eyes filled with horror as his life saving air whooshed down the tube. He grabbed for it, and Red moved it out of his reach. Armstrong looked on in sickened amazement. The air pocket grew smaller and the hundreds of smaller, individual bubbles rushed towards the intake. Loon began to go crazy as he started sucking in water. He tried to jack-knife down towards them but couldn't, his eyes rolled upwards, he seemed to be trying to shout out, then he began to really breathe water, his movements slowing down as he drowned.

Tina watched the two men surface and clamber into the boat. Tears filled her eyes, she tried to control the aching lump in her throat but couldn't and broke down into uncontrollable sobs of utter relief. She watched the boat approaching the jetty and bit her hand to stifle the sobs. She pulled a Kleenex from the glove compartment and blew her nose and wiped her eyes as they climbed the stone steps.

'What happened?' she almost shouted, dying to fall into the rubber clad arms of Red Angus, but shows of affection were still difficult in front of Jack.

'There'll be no more trouble from them,' Red gasped, sitting down. They were breathing heavily still. Her eyes searched them frantically for tell-tale signs of a fight. She'd been imagining the worst, all kind of bloody mental pictures.

'What happened?' she whispered again.

'They're dead down there,' Jack said, 'let's not go into detail, it was sickening.'

'Sickening? Hell, we've got it made now,' Red said, unzipping the wet rubber and unsnapping the buttons under his crotch.

'From the sounds in that airlift tube I think we've made contact with the bulk of the treasure.' Jack said.

'Oh, please God,' she said, 'God, let's hope so, I just want to end this whole episode of my life.'

'Yes, life was so pretty in Aberdeen wasn't it sweetheart.'

She glared at Armstrong with fury, his words cutting into her.

A half hour later they were gazing down at the gold. A big pile of dark green, mossy flat objects. They picked them up at random, pushing off the stinking wet mould and exposing the glittering gold, from coin after coin.

'Oh, what a wee sight,' Red mumbled with joy, he picked them up one by one, 'look at these five-guinea pieces… Queen Anne 1711.'

Tina took one looking at it closely, 'you're very clever.'

Red showed her, pointing to the tail side of one of the coins, 'look, four crowned escutcheons in the form of a cross, flanked by four sceptres with the garter in the middle.'

'Here's something different,' she said handing him another coin.

'Yes, George II 1727… five-guinea again.'

'Didn't expect English coins,' Jack ventured, 'I thought they would all be French, Bonnie Prince Charlie brought his treasure with him from France, didn't he?'

'Yes,' Red agreed, 'but look at this lot here, most of them are the Double Louis d'or. They were also called 'aw bandeau,' see the Kings head wearing the bandeau.'

'Well you really do know your coins.' Jack said.

'Like I said, the legend of the gold is part of life on Loch Ness. This gold has been on my mind for a very long time.'

Two hours later they'd hosed down the fantastic haul and knelt around the glittering mass of coins. Once Jack made a two-handed grab at the pile, sinking his fingers deep and lifting the coins and letting them trickle through his fingers in a sparkling cascade.

'No,' Red snapped, 'I know it's a great temptation, but that scratches the coins, the better the condition, the more they'll be worth.'

'But that's the one thing I've been dreaming of doing since I first heard of Charlie's Gold.' Armstrong laughed.

Tina found herself incapable of savouring the joy of the find. She felt nothing but foreboding. Her thoughts were with the dead men below and she couldn't believe their troubles were over.

'Let's hide this lot now,' she said, 'never know who might come along.'

They packed the coins carefully in a sports bag between many layers of newspaper.

'Okay, let's get the hell outta here.' Armstrong said, placing the bag in the rear of the beetle.

'We'll stash it at my campsite.' Red growled.

'You sure that's safe?' Jack asked.

'None safer laddie, there are many hiding places there.'

The sharp crack of a pine twig startled them. They turned to see the two men. Two big men. One in ex-army surplus fatigues, the other in tee-shirt, black leather jacket and Levi's.

197

One sported an over and under 12-bore, the other, in army gear, a single barrel pump action repeating shotgun.

'Hi.'

'Hello, can we help you?' Red greeted, as casual as he could.

'We're looking for Loon and Charlie Barsh, friends of ours.'

'We know them but haven't seen them for a couple of days.'

'Funny?' The one in the leather jacket said, sauntering onto the jetty and peering into the car.

'But you've been diving with them only today.' The other said.

All three of them now knew that their worst fears were being realised. The Barshes must have sent for these men.

'Yeah, that's right, we have.' Red grunted.

Their next words hammered into their brains, freezing their hearts. 'Nice little haul you have there.'

'What you mean?' Red asked nonchalantly.

'Don't give me any of that fucking crap,' the man with the repeater hissed, 'now I'll say it again, only this time you answer me correctly.'

He repeated the words. 'Nice little haul you have there.'

'Go screw yourself.' Red growled, his head down.

The man took the three steps he needed to reach Red Angus, then he brought his gun butt up in a scything arc to connect with the Scotsman's jaw. The sickening crunch resounded in the still air and Red staggered backwards three steps, fell to his haunches, tried to recover, then his senses left him and he sprawled backwards unconscious, hitting the back of his head on the flagstones of the jetty.

Tina screamed hysterically throwing herself onto the prostrate Red Angus, 'You bastards, you've killed him.'

'Not yet darling, not yet.' The man smirked.

Jack stood frozen to the spot, his head spinning.

'Do you want it next pretty boy?' the other man shouted.

'What you after?' Jack asked.

'We're after decent responses to what we ask.'

'Alright,' Jack snarled, 'alright, yeah, it is a nice little haul,' tears of rage welling in his eyes.

'Come on, let's have a look,' the man in the fatigues stepped forward nudging Jack with his gun butt. Jack looked down at Red who was kneeling, his head in his hands, a thin thread of red saliva hanging from his mouth and nose.

'Baby… you okay?' Tina asked, her arm round his hunched shoulders.

'Hmmm…' he looked up to see Armstrong leading the two men to the back seat of the Volkswagen.

'You take that, and we'll call the police.' He shouted.

'Take your choice,' Armstrong said. 'trouble with the law or a chance to see how much more is down there. That's just the first haul. Reckon it's a fraction of the main bulk,' he lied. They had already decided that they had more than likely vacuumed up most of the gold. They had continued until the rattling in the airlift pipe had stopped. First there had been the loud whooshing rattling sound when they had made contact with the main bulk of gold, then there was the gradual lessening of the sound until the rattling ceased. Then they continued until there was no more of that golden rattle. They were sure they had sucked up all but a handful of coins, the whole of Charlie's Gold.

The man hesitated at Armstrong's suggestion, and glanced at his mate.

'You got no idea where the two Barsh brothers are?'

'We told you,' Jack said, 'none at all.'

'You're just going to have to get the rest up today then, we'll just hang around.'

'God, they can't go down there again!' Tina choked.

'I don't think they got much of a choice darling, don't worry, we'll look after you while your boyfriends do the work.'

'Give us a couple of hours,' Jack said. 'it's rough down there.' He walked over and knelt beside Red. The big Scotsman seemed little worse for the blow, except for some blood and a swollen lip. 'You okay?'

'Yeah, yeah, don't worry,' Red whispered, spitting more blood.

'I'll get that brazier lit.' Jack said.

'Gimme a dram.'

Tina got Red's hip flask from the car and poured him a drink. Red winced as the neat whisky scorched the raw insides of his mouth.

'How much time you gonna need to rest up?' one of them asked.

Jack looked at his watch, it was already 2.30pm.

'Give us a couple of hours, we'll dive at 4.30.'

'You're stalling, you'll dive at 3.30, in an hour.'

The three watched the two men walk along the shore for twenty yards and settle down on the shingle of a sunny cove.

'No funny business now,' the man with the over and under, shouted back at them. 'this thing's got a pretty tight pattern at twenty yards,' he laughed and pointed to his gun muzzles. Red spat some more blood.

'Give me half a chance with a gun now and you'll be sunbathing in hell.' He whispered hoarsely almost to himself.

'What are you going to do?' Jack asked.

'For God's sake, no more killing, please!' she pleaded.

'We're going to have to take turns diving alone,' Red said. 'no way can we leave that gold up here while both of us go down.'

'But why go down again?' Armstrong asked. 'We've got every last coin.'

'To stall until tonight, if we tell them there's no more gold down there, they'll fuck off with the lot now. We'll pretend to dive for it for another hour then call it a day. We'll have all tonight to plan what to do.'

CHAPTER FOURTEEN

He found the swim down to the tunnel entrance much more difficult this time. He realised as he kicked awkwardly downwards that he hadn't fully recovered from the morning's dive. Some inexorable force was urging him down, drawing him towards the horror below.

As he approached the bottom, he suddenly became aware the tunnel entrance was obscured by considerable water disturbance. A large area of loch bottom around the tunnel entrance was a billowing mass of churned up muck. Then he thought he saw something, a movement in the murk, a big dark shape. Something was still there or had just entered or left the tunnel.

He stopped kicking, hovered and looked about him. Cold fear began to grip him. He waited for what seemed like five minutes, then a movement again, this time in the darkness to his right. He peered through the gloom and thought he saw a shape moving, a heavy, very long shape, at least thirty feet. He looked around him and saw other shapes. Then another massive dark form horrifyingly huge. He could see the rippling flanks, the fins. He gasped into his mouthpiece as he realised what was happening. He guessed that the two corpses in the cave were being devoured, and the scent was attracting them from every direction. He thought of himself, in his predicament, alone in the depths of Loch Ness. The world was still searching for its Loch Ness monster, its Nessie. The world was still making its jokes about the famous mythical monster, and here he was, alone in the dark with more monsters than he could count.

He asked himself what the hell he was doing there, playacting. They'd found the gold after all. A sense of awful desolation had closed around him. He wondered if all human beings felt like this before death. His senses had sharpened incredibly. He could hear his own heartbeat, taste the blood in his sinuses.

The big monster to his right had begun to move towards him.

Its flanks rippling with excitement, its jaws and gills working faster as it slid through the murk towards him. He adjusted the line around his waist and looked up to see it disappearing towards the light, towards light and warmth and life. Towards sunlight and happiness, a long time ago. A little boy in the safety of his mother's arms.

'I know you from somewhere don't I?' he said to her and handed her another Vodka.

She had begun to feel the pleasant effect of the alcohol and accepted the new drink. 'Cheers,' she said and tipped the drink down her throat. That was her sixth large Vodka. She needed the familiar numbing sensations to take her away from the nightmare reality of her predicament.

They were both sitting in the front of the Volkswagen, waiting and watching for Armstrong to surface, and watching Red Angus in the boat with the other man, she could see sunlight glint on his shotgun barrel. 'Yeah, I expect you do,' she was already slurring, 'I expect you screwed me once.'

'Wha...'

'Aberdeen... that's where I come from... where I used to work. If you come from Aberdeen you most definitely screwed me,' she said spilling drink down her tee-shirt.

'Shit, of course, I remember!' his face lit up.

'Sssh…' she put two fingers to his lips, 'don't tell me, I'm trying to forget. If you screwed me you screwed me, I just don't wanna know the details okay? 'You see, I'm a good girl now, I'm in love.'

'No, I didn't screw you, but I remember, you're a stripper.'

'Was darling, was a stripper, and a whore.'

'Come here you,' he said, grabbing her by the arm and pulling her towards him. 'Come sit on my lap.'

She moved across the front seat, 'another drink please sir.' She said holding out her empty glass. She was in a world of her own now, back in Aberdeen, in the club, on the lap of one of her admirers, and the drinks were flowing.

She sat holding onto the dashboard as he held her under her blouse. She moaned, 'You bastard.'

Red Angus knelt in the boat, both hands on the blue nylon rope still playing it out from the coil laid out neatly in the bottom of the boat. The man with the pump-action gun knelt beside him, watching his every move.

Jack moved again, downwards towards the dark gash in the loch floor, now just visible as the murk cleared. He was aware he needn't go any further but an inexorable compulsion had taken hold…

The huge creature had slid up behind, within a couple of feet. Now the human scent was too much. Its flanks and ruffed dorsal were rippling with anticipation. The rows of teeth were bared, the gills distended, nearly thirty feet of prehistoric savagery. Another strong smell permeated through his face mask, the same smell that he remembered from that first sighting from the bank of the loch. His thoughts went back to that happy morning, those first idyllic days with her. He turned and found himself looking into the maw of death itself. The eel launched itself, hitting him with open mouthed fury, carrying him backwards with the incredible impact of attack.

She squealed as she felt his hands on her bare breasts and fought to control her alcohol sodden brain. She tried to focus on Red Angus through the windscreen. What was he doing out there, she thought she was sitting on his lap, thought she was feeling his hands under her tee-shirt, him under her squirming hips. For Heaven's sake!

The long panga came up from behind, from the rear seat. The small hard hand, skin tight over the knuckles, holding the snake entwined skull handle.

In a flash it was drawing across his neck, biting deep, the windpipe and jugular gurgling as blood gushed, splashing warmly over her back and spraying across the windscreen. She saw the blood, heard it coming, felt the warm wetness splash down her back, saw lots of it down the front of her tee-shirt. Her brain was too numbed, but she screamed, instinct telling her to run. She fumbled with the door, tumbled out of the car and began to stagger along the jetty.

Armstrong died immediately. Now the huge fish was moving away fast through the weed jungle with the corpse firmly locked in its jaws, the rope trailing, moving away from the other monsters that were beginning to close in.

Red dropped the rope and turned to see the staggering blood drenched Tina as she tottered on the edge of the jetty. The gunman stood legs astride to keep balance in the rocking boat and raised his shotgun. 'Fuck… what the fuck's going on?' Red shouted. Then he opened up the throttle and the little boat lifted its nose and gunned towards the jetty.

Tina could see the boat pitching towards her, Red Angus standing up in the boat, her vision blurred, her senses wrecked with vodka.

The boat hit the jetty head on. 'Red… Red!' Tina screamed as the boat collided with the stone structure.

She jumped headlong into the boat and into Red Angus's arms. The boat rocked dangerously, water gushing over the gunwales.

The gunman leaped onto the jetty, the car was well within shotgun range, he could see Frazer's face framed in the rear window of the car, he could see the windscreen drenched in red and through the driver's window he could see his partner sitting with his head lolling on his left shoulder.

All this he saw in the split second before he raised his shotgun to his shoulder. Red Angus and Tina, still in the boat watched in horror, they saw Whitie's face frozen in the car window, a portrait of horror. The gunman jerked off both barrels and the portrait exploded, the car rocking on its suspension with the impact. Whitie moaned, he knew there was not much left of his face, he couldn't see and knew that his one good eye was destroyed. He could feel lead shot deep in his brain, but incredibly he was conscious. He fumbled in his darkness, his bloody hands searching, clawing, then he found it. His right hand closed on the ivory of the snake entwined skull handle.

Red Angus, Tina and the gunman watched as the car door opened and the blood drenched apparition staggered out onto the jetty. The gunman gasped in horror, took a couple of backward steps and dropped two more cartridges into his breech.

Whitie stood there for a couple of seconds, his mashed face tilted upwards, unseeing in the attitude of a blind man, he raised the panga, tilted his head back further, then he made the african curse come true, his life blood shining brightly in the afternoon sunlight, his long and traumatic life at an end.

Red Angus stood in the boat with Tina, in frozen horror at the scene while down in the bottom of the boat the slowly moving coils of nylon rope, still attached to Armstrong's corpse, tightened round Tina's ankle. She gasped as the vice-like grip jerked her leg, suddenly wrenching her from his arms.

Red saw the rope snapping taut with the sound of a rifle crack, taut from at least hundred yards out into the Loch, catapulting her backwards and dragging her under the water surface. Red's hoarse shout of despair was cut short as he flung himself headlong into the loch after her. He swam with all his strength, downwards, clawing deeper and deeper, his eyes smarting, non-seeing with no mask. He found the rope, quivering and jerking, and pulled himself downwards along it, then his lungs, hurting, feeling like bursting. He knew he wouldn't make it any further. The pain in his chest hammered inside him, his ears pounded. He heard himself cry out in the water… in despair, in panic for her. He turned and pushed to the surface, then made for the jetty, struggling, kicking awkwardly in exhaustion. He hauled himself onto the stonework and lay there on his stomach, searching frantically over the loch surface, no sign.

He saw the gunman still standing there, looking stunned. 'You fucking bastard, you just wait there, I will be back for you!' his words choked on his sobs. Then he was pulling on his flippers, humping on the scuba tanks. He was back in the water with his face mask still in his hand. He cleared the mask and was diving again, this time with air and clear sight. He could see the quivering rope stretching down into the depths, it continued down, just taut, but still playing out from the boat. Soon he began to feel the pressure, he cleared his ears and continued, still further. Daylight was diminishing now as he realised he was heading for the great depths of the loch. He kicked on a little further, then he knew there could be no more hope. He could see the rope going down almost vertically. He hovered there, holding the rope, his cheek against it, then the tears came, under his mask, and he cried. He sobbed with grief, then he sobbed with rage. He could feel the anger rising from the pit of his stomach as he kicked upwards.

He broke surface among the reeds that fringed the jetty wall, out of sight of the gunman standing above. Pulling off the face mask and flippers and shrugging off his air tanks he moved silently onto the bank. Then the sound came to him, a far-off sound at first, then stronger as it came nearer. A siren, police or fire brigade.

He swore softly. They mustn't rob him of his vengeance, he must kill, kill for Tina, the bastards had murdered her just when he'd found her. He wept again, his sobbing full of grief and hate. Now there was another siren, they were coming in force.

He wondered if anyone had witnessed the scenes of a few minutes ago, someone must have called the police, fire brigade, ambulances. He'd have to get the bastard quick.

He reached the VW and peered under the wheels. The gunman was searching the water, gun ready, agitated. Red opened the rear door of the car and saw what was inside. He gagged at the sight, so much blood, and the smell, the familiar smell of a butcher's shop but more intense.

The man sitting in the front seat was seated upright, but his head hung backwards over his left shoulder, his eyes were looking upside down at Red. The long musket, and the bag of cartridges were still lying on the car floor.

The sirens were loud now, there were many vehicles and they seemed to be coming from all directions, there was a couple of minutes at the most.

Bite the cartridge, prime the pan, ramrod, ram. The gunman was panicking now, coming towards the car. Ten yards, five yards, he was running. There must be no missing, no misfiring… only one shot.

Red stood up and saw the look of terror in the man's eyes as he brought the long gun up and squeezed off his shot. The heavy ball slammed full into the man's face somersaulting him backwards into eternity.

He could hear the screeches of brakes and the slamming of many car doors. Throwing the musket down he wrenched open the car door again. The bag of gold was still there on the rear seat, he leaned in and grabbed it. Then he was running for his life, up the hill and into the timber. In the next few seconds Ruthven Jetty and its surroundings was swarming with humanity.

The big Harley Davidson was waiting in the layby. It roared into life at the first kick and he was away, throttle full open, the wind in his face whipping the tears back across the sides of his face and into his hair. He was shouting into the rushing wind, shouting with grief and despair.

The 'Queen of the Loch' chugged happily along in mid-loch. She looked good in her shining new paint. Blue hull and pristine white bridge and superstructure. Her name proudly sparkled in gold on her prow. A thirty-foot banner along both her rails proclaimed her expedition… TWO HOUR NESSIE SPOTTING TRIP.

Timmy sat in the prow, his head through the rails. Like his mum and dad and all the other passengers, his eyes were glued to the loch surface. Ever ready binoculars and cameras were in abundance. 'The Queen' had shown hundreds of her passengers the basking Nessie over the years. The skipper up on the bridge squinted into the sunlight, hoping like he'd hoped on the last trip and the one before, that this trip would be one of the lucky ones. It was good for business when sightings were frequent.

Timmy gazed out over the sparkling surface, screwing his eyes and nose up against the sun's rays refracting off the water. An hour had already gone by since they had set off from the mooring at Fort Augustus. He wanted to go back to school with an exciting story to tell his friends about the monster he'd seen, he started wishing.

'I wish, I wish, I wish I… mum, mum, what's that?' he was pointing.

Mum's and Dad's and everybody else's eyes were on the boy, staring at the loch in the direction of his pointing finger. The skipper sensed the sudden excitement on the deck below and picked up his binoculars.

A dark shape, definitely something out there, about hundred yards to starboard. He soon picked up the shape and focused the glasses.

The woman was floating on her back. Her face, shoulders and chest visible above the surface.

'Get back now… for God's sake, move back, get these people back.'

'Is she dead?'

'It's a woman…'

'She's alive.'

'She's still alive,' the skipper shouted, hold back everybody, for God's sake she needs some air.'

Her eyelids flickered and she murmured, then heaved and belched as the man sitting astride her back pressed down hard on her shoulder blades and water and alcohol spewed from her mouth.

'She's going to make it.'

'I thought she was the monster,' little Timmy grumbled disappointedly.

CHAPTER FIFTEEN

The vision clad in white moved into focus and hovered over her. 'You nearly drowned,' the young nurse whispered, 'but you're alright now. You are lucky you got away with just a broken ankle.'

'What happened?' she mumbled terrified, vague images of horror tore at her subconscious.

'For God's sake what happened, the people I was with, where?'

'Calm down, calm down,' she felt the cool soft hand on her forehead.

'God I must find out, Red, Red!'

That evening at nine o'clock she plugged herself into the radio news.

The first item told her.

'There was a shooting incident this morning on the banks of Loch Ness. Police arrived on the scene to find the dead bodies of two men. Police at first suspected a gangland killing as both dead men are known criminals from Aberdeen and Glasgow. However, it has now emerged that four other men and a young woman are also connected. These people are missing, and the police have launched a massive search for the five. The man who ventured the information which has set the police on this course is a young American, Jimmy Bell, who manages the Loch Ness Zoological Bureau, an organisation dedicated to the search of the Loch Ness monster.'

She listened in horror as the American voice of Bell came

over the air.

'Yes, I'd got to know them well since they came to camp on the loch. Their names are Tina and Jack, I'm sorry I don't know their surnames, and Red Angus, a very well-known loch-side character. They started off searching for the creature, but after a while became obsessed with Charlie's Gold. I know they had a hunch of some sort and were taking it very seriously, they'd started to dive. They'd become involved with the Barsh brothers and had become very concerned. They had received a few threatening overtures.'

'Barsh brothers?' the interviewer asked.

'Yes, two men who were also searching for the gold.' Answered Bell.

She knew the police would come.

CHAPTER SIXTEEN

A whole month had passed since her admittance to hospital. They'd told her that her foot had nearly been torn off at the ankle. There had been interminable questioning about how the accident had happened. The police did come, many times, but there was nothing she could tell them. Arrangements had been made to take her to police headquarters for even further questioning on the day she was due out. She decided not to wait for that day. As soon as she was able to walk, she escaped.

The ankle had healed... more or less. There had been many stitches, torn ligaments and a compound fracture. She was indeed lucky to be walking along this mountain roadside. Death must have come very close that day, she thought. The ankle and foot were still heavily plastered and bandaged. She knew she should have really given herself more time, the ankle more time to strengthen. But there had been no choice. The pain was almost unbearable now with every step.

From what she could remember she was almost there. She could see the sea again now, hear its distant crashing against the rocks far below.

She had given up trying to remember the horrors of Ruthven Jetty. There were vague and misty images like some long-forgotten nightmare. She could remember nothing, some awful calamity, but that's all. No memory of that frightful head-long plunge into the depths, no memory of that awful throat cutting, nothing. She limped painfully up the ridge, dragging her right foot behind her.

She reached the crest and the fantastic vista of sea and sky presented itself.

She'd been on the road for two pain filled days. She had hitched lifts for most of the way, but there were no more lifts in this beautiful remoteness.

The wind whipped at her as she approached the cliff edge and walked towards the small green painted sign that pointed the way down the cliff side.

She looked out over the turquoise waves, eyes searching, the wind forcing tears from them. She peeled the hair from her face, eyes still searching, straining to see against the backdrop of spray flecked waves. Then she saw them, a group of them, white bodies, wings black tipped. They were flying low over the waves. She saw one, then two, then three soar upwards, hang for a second, then wings folded like giant arrowheads, they plummeted into the heaving ocean only to appear seconds later, a struggle for lift off, then climb into the air again to search some more.

Looking down at the tiny natural harbour far below, her eyes searched among the rocks on the beach, nestling under the massive cliffs. She wiped her streaming eyes with the palms of her hands and searched again, trying to distinguish light and shade, form and colour. She saw the tiny little rectangular speck of blue, the tent, tight against the irregular lines of the ruined cottage. She could see the stone chimney, and the wisp of blue smoke. Her gaze moved along and onto the stone pier.

The minuscule figure was standing at the end of the pier. She knew what he was doing, knew he was concentrating, his eyes fixed on the little orange float that was dancing in the swirling eddy in the rocks.

Her eyes were full of tears again, as she began to run down the rock steps. She looked out to sea again. The birds were still there, wheeling over the waves… the westering sun painting their wings. She started to run down the steps again… nothing hurt anymore.

THE END